STEPHANIE

Stephanie's planning a big party at her house with D.J. as the chaperone. Stephanie invites tons of people from school and buys lots of snacks and drinks. But when D.J. realizes she *can't* chaperone, Stephanie has to cancel the party and *un*invite all her guests.

Too bad she couldn't get in touch with everyone, because on Friday night, tons of kids come to her house! Stephanie realizes that she's having a party whether she wants to or not. And when unwanted guests show up, Stephanie knows trouble isn't far behind.

MICHELLE

Michelle is excited to help with Stephanie's party. But as she's looking for decorations, she finds something even more exciting. A clue in an old diary that leads to a hidden treasure—in her very own house!

Michelle searches high and low, tearing apart the contents of closets and storage spaces. Will Michelle and her friends be able to find the treasure? Or will they just find that they've made a humongous mess?

FULL HOUSE™: SISTERS books

Two on the Town
One Boss Too Many
And the Winner Is . . .
How to Hide a Horse
Problems in Paradise
Will You Be My Valentine?
Let's Put On a Show!
Baby-sitters and Company
Substitute Sister
Ask Miss Know-It-All
Matchmakers
No Rules Weekend
A Dog's Life
  (coming in April 2001)

Available from MINSTREL Books

FULL HOUSE™
Sisters

No Rules Weekend

BRAD AND BARBARA STRICKLAND

A Parachute Press Book

A MINSTREL® BOOK

Published by POCKET BOOKS
New York   London   Toronto   Sydney   Singapore

A MINSTREL PAPERBACK *Original*

A Minstrel Book published by
POCKET BOOKS, a division of Simon & Schuster, Inc.
1230 Avenue of the Americas, New York, NY 10020

A PARACHUTE PRESS BOOK

Copyright © and ™ 2001 by Warner Bros.

FULL HOUSE, characters, names and all related indicia are trademarks of Warner Bros. © 2001.

ISBN: 0-671-04092-8

First Minstrel Books printing February 2001

10 9 8 7 6 5 4 3 2 1

A MINSTREL BOOK and colophon are registered trademarks of Simon & Schuster, Inc.

Printed in the U.S.A.

No Rules Weekend

MICHELLE

Chapter
1

Michelle Tanner shoved her father toward the front door. "*Good-bye*, Dad," she said for the fourth time that morning.

"Now, you have my pager number—" Danny Tanner began. He spoke to Michelle's eighteen-year-old sister, D.J. D.J. stood behind Michelle, leaning against the door frame.

"I have your pager number, your cell phone number, Aunt Becky's cell phone number, the numbers of both of your rooms at the hotel . . ." D.J. interrupted. "I've got every possible number I could need. Please don't worry, Dad. The three of us will be fine here. You're only going to be away for a few days."

Michelle nodded. "She's right, Dad," she said.

"I don't know," Danny mumbled. He still looked worried. He ran a hand through his dark hair. "I really hate to leave you three girls all alone in the house over the weekend. If Joey hadn't gotten a chance to fill in at that comedy show in Las Vegas . . ."

"But he did," Michelle pointed out.

"It was a great opportunity," D.J. added. "He had to take it. And you and Becky have an assignment to tape a segment of your TV show in Los Angeles. And Uncle Jesse wants to go along and take the twins. So that leaves Steph, Michelle, me, and Comet here on our own." The Tanners' dog, Comet, came up beside D.J. at the sound of his name. She ruffled his ears. "We've got a perfectly good watchdog. He'll keep us safe. And we'll do fine. Trust me."

"It's not that I don't trust you," Danny told her. "I just hate to go off and leave you alone and in charge like this."

2

Michelle tugged at his sports jacket. She said, "Dad, I'm really, really going to miss you this weekend. But I can't start missing you until you go away."

Michelle felt D.J.'s hands on her shoulders. "We'll be perfectly all right, Dad," D.J. said. "Really."

From the street the girls' uncle Jesse shouted, "Hey, Danny! Hurry up! The taxi's waiting!"

Danny smiled. "Okay, okay. Guess I'll have to stop being overprotective." He picked up his small suitcase and turned toward the front door. Then he turned back and set his suitcase down again. "Wait a minute, where's Stephanie?"

Michelle rolled her eyes. Would her dad ever stop worrying so much? "She's in the kitchen, making our breakfast," she said. "You know that. She already said good-bye to you—*twice*."

"Right, right," Danny said, taking a deep breath. "Well, I guess I ought to go." Michelle noticed that he didn't move.

"Dad, I'm eighteen now," D.J. reminded

him. "Don't you remember how responsible *you* were at eighteen?"

"Maybe he wasn't very responsible then. Maybe that's why he doesn't want to leave," Michelle teased.

Danny laughed. "All right. You win. Give me a hug, you two." He wrapped his arms around the two of them. "I'll call every night to make sure you're okay," Danny promised. He picked up his suitcase and made it out the door—finally. "Be good, girls!" he added over his shoulder.

Michelle and D.J. watched from the porch as their dad made his way to the curb. It was a beautiful, warm Thursday morning in San Francisco. Danny put his suitcase in the trunk of the taxi. At last, he climbed in with Uncle Jesse, Aunt Becky, and the twins. The car roared away as Michelle and D.J. waved good-bye.

Michelle turned and walked back inside. Almost at once she realized that she could hear little sounds she had never noticed before. A clock ticked upstairs. A bird twittered outside the front windows. From the

4

kitchen came the click of the toaster. The Tanner house was peaceful and quiet. Of course, that wasn't a bad thing, but it sure seemed weird. Usually the place was anything but silent, because it was crowded with a whole bunch of people!

Michelle's mother had died when Michelle was just a baby—and Danny thought he needed lots of help raising his three daughters. He asked his best friend, Joey Gladstone, to move in. He also asked the girls' uncle, Jesse. The two lived with Michelle, her dad, and her sisters as one big, happy family.

Then Uncle Jesse married Rebecca Donaldson, Danny's partner on *Wake Up, San Francisco*, the TV show they hosted together. Jesse and Becky had changed part of the attic into a cozy apartment. Now they lived there with their twin boys, Alex and Nicky. That made nine people in one very full house. Comet, the Tanners' golden retriever, made ten!

Michelle thought it was fun to have so many people around. Sure, the place could get crazy, and sometimes she had to wait a long time to get into a bathroom. But life at the Tanners' was never dull. Something was *always* going on!

D.J. leaned against the closed front door. "I didn't think they'd ever leave," she said.

"Yeah," Michelle agreed. "Does Dad think we're babies or something?"

"He's a dad," D.J. reminded her sister. "If he's not worried about us, he's not happy." She took a blue scrunchie from her jeans pocket and pulled her long blond hair into a ponytail.

Michelle took hold of D.J.'s wrist so she could look at her sister's watch. "Five, four, three . . ." she counted down.

"What are you doing?" D.J. asked with a smile.

"Waiting for Dad's first phone call," Michelle replied. "He's probably punching our number into his cell phone right now. Two." She paused. "One . . ."

Only a second later the phone rang. From the kitchen, fourteen-year-old Stephanie yelled, "Could someone please answer that? I'm cooking!"

"Got it," D.J. called. She picked up the receiver. "Hello?" She paused and winked at Michelle. "Oh, hi, Dad."

Michelle rolled her eyes in an exaggerated way. *Do I know Dad, or do I know Dad?* she thought with a little glow of satisfaction. She listened in on D.J.'s side of the conversation. Its general tone was pretty clear.

"Right. I'll remember to do that," D.J. promised. "Yes, of course I know when Michelle's bedtime is. Yes, I'll be sure the front door is locked. Don't worry. No, we have plenty of groceries. Yes, I have the money you left. No, we don't need anything. Okay, talk to you tonight. Love you, too. Have fun in L.A."

"Breakfast is served!" Stephanie announced from the kitchen. "Hurry before it gets cold!"

"I really have to go, Dad," D.J. declared. "No, nothing's wrong. It's just breakfast, that's all. Okay. Bye, now." She hung up the receiver, shaking her head.

In the kitchen Michelle saw that Stephanie had everything ready.

"I think this is a pretty good breakfast,"

Stephanie said proudly. "Even if I did make it myself." She poured a glass of milk for Michelle.

"Mmm—crispy and steamy. Way to pop toaster waffles, Steph." Michelle reached for the maple syrup and a fork.

For a while the three sisters ate in silence. Michelle began to feel strange. Something was sort of bugging her, even though she couldn't figure out what it was. She thought about it as she ate and finally realized her problem. "Boy, this place is quiet," she commented a little too loudly.

Stephanie drank the last of her milk. "Absolutely," she agreed. "Usually you can't hear yourself think in the mornings. Everyone's running around getting ready for school or work. It's nice to have some peace and quiet for a change."

D.J. collected the dirty plates and headed for the sink. "The whole place seems a lot bigger, too," she remarked over her shoulder. "At breakfast time you usually can't turn around in the kitchen."

Michelle nodded. "And everyone's in a

8

hurry. We've got plenty of time this morning."

D.J. set the dishes in the sink and glanced at her watch. "You're right. I've got half an hour before I have to leave for college. Are you two ready for school? I'll give you a lift."

"Thanks," Stephanie answered. Her eyes gave a mischievous twinkle.

Uh-oh, Michelle thought. *I've seen that look before. It usually means that Stephanie's got some kind of crazy plan!*

Stephanie went on, "We can leave as soon as we discuss my latest, most brilliant idea."

D.J. turned toward her. "Brilliant, huh? What is it?" she asked. Her eyes narrowed in suspicion.

"This isn't about painting our room lime green, is it?" Michelle demanded. "Because that was *my* idea!"

"Whoa! Hold it!" D.J. shouted. "First of all, Michelle, no one's painting anything this weekend. Activities like that have to be Dad-approved, and—"

"Relax. My idea's nothing like that," Stephanie promised. "We all think the house feels empty—and we've got so much room here. So let's fill it up."

"With what?" Michelle asked.

"With friends!" Stephanie cheered. "Let's have a party!"

Michelle blinked. A party? That sounded like major fun.

"No way, Steph," D.J. insisted. "Dad left me in charge, and I don't want to get in trouble with him."

"There won't *be* any trouble," Stephanie argued, "because Dad already told me that I could have some friends over. He promised weeks and weeks ago. But I could never find a good time for a party. Until now."

"That's true," Michelle reported to D.J. "I remember when Dad told Steph she could have a party. It was about a month ago."

Stephanie nodded. "But he was always too busy. So this is the perfect chance," she continued. "We've got the house all to ourselves. We could have an awesome party tomorrow night. And that would give us all day Saturday to clean up—not that there would be much of a mess."

D.J. looked doubtful. "Who would come to this party?" she asked Stephanie.

Good question, Michelle thought. She was wondering that herself.

Stephanie shrugged. "Just some of my closest friends. Not all that many. I mean, not a *mob* or anything."

D.J. crossed her arms and frowned. "You want to invite a houseful of fourteen-year-olds?"

"Not a *houseful,*" Stephanie replied. "Just a few friends. And not even all of my friends. Just enough to have a little fun, that's all."

That seems pretty cool! Michelle thought. *As long as I don't have to stay in my room.* She gave D.J. a pleading look.

D.J. seemed to understand it. "What about Michelle?" she asked.

"She can be at the party," Stephanie promised. "And Mandy and Cassie, too."

"Yes!" Michelle punched the air with her fist. She knew that she and her best friends would have a great time. "Can we have the party, D.J.? Please?"

Stephanie smiled at her and then at D.J. "It's not going to be wild and crazy. Just some friends, some music, some food. It will be totally fun. Come on, D.J."

"Well . . ." D.J. said hesitantly.

"Say yes," Michelle urged. "Nothing can go wrong. I'll keep an eye on everything!" She paused. "Plus, you'll be here, too."

"Good point," Stephanie put in. "D.J., you'll be the chaperone. You're mature. I mean, that's why Dad trusts you to watch us for the weekend. With you at the party, what could happen?"

After a moment's pause, D.J. sighed. "I'm probably going to regret this," she said with a smile. "But okay."

"Yay!" Michelle yelled. "Par-tay!" She and Stephanie slapped each other a high five.

"Omigosh, we have to start planning!" Stephanie exclaimed. "We need lots of music and refreshments. D.J., can we borrow some of your coolest CDs? And I'll get the kids to bring some music, too. And, oh—decorations! We'll have to do some majorly serious decorating!"

"I'll help," Michelle told her. She couldn't stop smiling. Hanging out with Stephanie's friends would be totally awesome. They were all so cool. "What kind of decorations do you want?" she asked.

"I don't know," Stephanie murmured. "Let me think. We don't want anything lame. And we don't want to go overboard. Plus, we have to get ready for the party after school tomorrow, so we won't have much time. It has to be simple but funky and cool." She placed a finger on her lips, thinking. "Hey, I know. We could get out those lights from the attic—the extra Christmas ones Dad bought. He thought they were red, but they turned out to be pink. Remember?"

"Pink lights. Excellent. When do we start the rest of the planning?" Michelle asked.

"Maybe *after* school," D.J. said. She tapped her watch. "It's getting late."

"Okay." Stephanie laughed. "Let's grab our stuff, Michelle."

As she raced upstairs for her backpack, Michelle thought about how exciting the next couple of days would be. And not just because of the party.

Michelle had never gone into the attic—the *real* attic where the pink lights were stored.

Now she'd get to explore the whole thing. And she could just imagine how terrific the house would look after she and Steph decorated it.

Yup, it was going to be a totally fun weekend.

And nothing could *possibly* ruin it.

STEPHANIE

Chapter 2

Allie!" Stephanie called from her locker. "Darcy! I have awesome news!"

The halls of John Muir Middle School were packed with students getting ready for class. Allie and Darcy fought their way toward their lockers—right next to Stephanie's.

"What's up?" Allie asked as soon as they got close enough to talk.

"You're not going to believe this!" Stephanie exclaimed. "I am throwing the coolest party ever—at my house tomorrow night."

Allie and Darcy glanced at each other.

"Oh. Okay," Darcy said.

Stephanie felt a little let down. "Well, you don't seem very excited about it," she pointed out.

Allie shrugged. "It's just that, well, a party in your parents' house is a party in your parents' house, you know?"

Darcy nodded in agreement. "Just when things start to really get fun, your dad will ask us to keep it down. Everyone's parents do."

"My dad won't," Stephanie insisted. She couldn't keep a mischievous grin from creeping onto her face. "He *can't!* He's not even in town. He's away for the weekend."

Darcy shrugged. "So? Your uncle Jesse or Joey will tell us to be quiet," she insisted. "Same difference."

Stephanie raised an eyebrow. "What if *they're* not home, either?"

"Wait a minute," Allie said, narrowing her eyes. "What exactly are you trying to tell us?"

"Okay," Stephanie said. "This is going to be so cool. And you guys have to help me invite everyone."

With students jostling past her on their way

to homeroom, Stephanie quickly filled in her two friends. "So with everyone gone, D.J. said we can have the party. She'll be the chaperone," she finished.

"Everyone's *gone* except for you and your sisters?" Darcy asked in a delighted, surprised voice. A big grin spread across her face. "No way!"

"Way!" Stephanie told them, shutting her locker. "It's just me, Michelle, and D.J. D.J. is going to be a great chaperone. She's very cool. She won't mind if we dance and turn the music up a little louder than normal."

"This is going to be great," Allie said. "We have to invite all the coolest guys we know."

"And I need you to help me decorate and decide on food," Stephanie added. "The house should look awesome, and we have to have great stuff to munch on. I'm thinking—"

The first bell for homeroom interrupted her. "Whoops!" she called as she started her homeroom dash. "Let's talk it over at lunch."

That morning seemed to drag by. Usually Stephanie could stay interested in her classes, but that Thursday her mind was full of music, food, and fun. She started to make a list of things to buy for the party. As she went from class to class, she asked a few people to come. Not very many—just five or ten close friends. And she let each one know it would be okay to bring one of their friends along, too.

Finally lunchtime arrived. Stephanie sat with Allie and Darcy in an uncrowded corner of the cafeteria.

"Fish sticks, ugh," Darcy groaned, poking at one with her fork. "There should be a federal law against these things."

Stephanie looked up from her grocery list. Allie had a strange twinkle in her eyes. "What's going on?" she asked.

Allie glanced at Darcy. "Think we should tell her?"

"Tell me what?" Stephanie said. "Have you two been up to something?"

Darcy dropped her fish stick and grinned. "Steph, you're gonna *die* when you hear this."

Allie leaned closer. "Who's by far the hunkiest guy in the entire school?" she whispered.

Stephanie felt her cheeks grow hot as she blushed. "Bobby Michaels?" she asked. *"That hunkiest guy in the school?"*

"Yep, Bobby Michaels is the correct answer," Allie replied with a triumphant smile. "And he's coming to your party!"

"You're kidding," Stephanie said. *"Aren't you?"*

Darcy and Allie just kept smiling at her.

Stephanie felt her heart beat a little faster. Of course Allie and Darcy knew that Stephanie had a crush on Bobby. Stephanie and her friends shared all their secrets. Bobby was tall, dark-haired, and handsome. He was very popular, too. He was one of the class officers and had a great sense of humor—not to mention the cutest grin. But Stephanie and Bobby had only one class together. They had hardly spoken to each other at all. What could she possibly talk to him about at the party?

"Did he really say he'd come?" Stephanie asked.

Darcy nodded. "He really did."

Stephanie sighed. *Bobby Michaels!* she thought. *I'll bet he's a wonderful dancer. Maybe he'll dance with me all through the party.* She began to daydream—

Allie interrupted her thoughts, yelling, "Duck!"

Stephanie didn't ask why. She ducked—just as a fish stick sailed over her head. "What—" she began. But she kept her head down as an apple flew through the air in the opposite direction.

"I'll give you one guess," Darcy said.

"Don't tell me," Stephanie said with a groan. "Mark Arnett and Steven Pascoe."

"Correct again," Allie told her.

Mark Arnett and Steven Pascoe were seventh graders. They weren't exactly bad guys. They were pretty nice, actually. But they could get a little wild. Whenever there was a food fight in the cafeteria or a water-balloon fight on the school lawn, it was a pretty sure thing that Mark and Steven had had something to do with it.

"Eeew!" Stephanie said, as a blob of gelatin splattered onto the table beside her.

"That's enough!" yelled the cafeteria's cashier. "Everyone settle down now. Mark, Steven, come with me!"

Stephanie and her friends sat up straight.

"Well, that was exciting," Stephanie said.

Allie rolled her eyes. "Those guys think they're so funny."

Darcy shrugged and grinned. "Hey, I was kind of tempted to chuck my fish sticks, too." She turned to Stephanie. "Speaking of food, what are you going to have to munch on at your party?"

"I've been thinking about that," Stephanie said. "At first I thought pizza, but it's gonna be a long evening. Pizza's great until the cheese gets cold and yucky!"

"Yeah, then it's a bummer," Darcy agreed. "What else is there? My mom serves those little cheese sandwiches with the crusts cut off at her parties."

"It's totally classy," Allie offered.

"Too much work," Stephanie decided. "And boys wouldn't even notice the effort. They, like, *inhale* food."

"So you need something they can't inhale," Allie mused. "Something substantial."

Stephanie snapped her fingers. "How about one of those humongous hero sandwiches?

They had a party at Dad's TV studio last year, and he brought home about three feet of Hoagie S. Grinder's Super Sub Special. Everyone loved it."

"How big do they make them?" Allie asked. "You don't want to wind up with two dozen feet of leftover sandwich."

"Plus it might be expensive," Darcy pointed out.

"Okay," Stephanie said, clicking her ballpoint pen. She started to write on her list. "Say we have twenty guests. If we ordered a five-foot sandwich, everyone would get a fourth of a foot. That's three inches of sandwich, which is perfect because those things are *packed!* And we can get chips and cookies—"

"And salsa and dip!" Allie put in.

"Exactly!" Stephanie wrote those down. "And we could—" She stopped when she felt Darcy poking her over and over in the arm. "What?" She followed Darcy's gaze, straight into the soft green eyes . . . of Bobby Michaels! He was standing right at their table!

"Hey, Steph," he said with a wide smile.

"Thanks for the invite. It's so cool that you're having a party when your parents aren't home."

Stephanie started to speak, but her vocal cords felt frozen. She cleared her throat. "We-we'll have an awesome time," she finally said.

"Well, I can't wait. See you tomorrow night." Bobby pointed at her, then walked away.

Stephanie blinked as she watched him make his way back across the lunchroom. *Wow!* she thought. *Did that really just happen? Bobby Michaels said he can't wait to see me!*

"Way to go, Stephanie," Darcy whispered.

"He can't wait," Stephanie repeated, still feeling a little dazed. "Maybe he likes me." She followed Bobby through the cafeteria with her gaze.

He stopped at another table. Stephanie's biology lab partner, Chrissy, was sitting there. Bobby slid into the empty seat beside her and started talking and laughing. He pointed at Stephanie, and Chrissy turned and waved.

Stephanie felt the smile fade from her face.

Bobby looked as if he really liked talking to Chrissy. She said something quietly to him—and he threw back his head and laughed.

Wait a minute, Stephanie thought. *Maybe the girl who Bobby really likes is Chrissy!*

"Earth to Stephanie," Allie said, nudging her. "We still have lots of planning to do for your party."

"And it's going to be great," Darcy added.

Stephanie nodded. Sure, it was. *And Bobby would have a great time. At the end of the night he'd have me to thank for that—not Chrissy!*

After school Stephanie, Darcy, and Allie called the Hoagie S. Grinder store. Stephanie asked about prices. Then she ordered a huge sandwich with all the trimmings.

After that the three girls went party shopping. It was totally fun. But it also cost more than Stephanie had planned to spend. She realized that all her allowance and baby-sitting savings were going to be used up. *Oh, well,* she decided, *if we have a great time, it's worth it.*

The bags of food and the two cases of sodas

were heavy. When Michelle opened the door of the Tanners' house for the loaded-down girls, her eyes widened. "Whoa! *Serious munchies!*"

"They're for the party," Stephanie reminded her. "Nobody opens them until tomorrow! What are you up to?"

"Cassie's mom drove us home, so now Cassie and Mandy are here," Michelle said. "We're gonna explore the attic and find those lights, okay?"

"Knock yourself out," Stephanie told her. "Allie, Darcy, and I will put away these goodies."

"Great. See you later," Michelle said. She raced upstairs.

Stephanie and her friends lugged the food to the kitchen.

"This party had better be worth all the fuss," Darcy said as she began unpacking a bag of chips and dips.

Allie wedged three gallons of ice cream in the freezer, and shrugged. "Even if it isn't, at least everyone will eat really well."

"No kidding." Stephanie began ticking items off her list, just to be sure that she had everything. "Pretzels, chips, dip, cookies, ice cream, candy, and plenty of sodas," she said. "We're stocked."

Darcy started to put boxes of cookies into a cabinet. "I'll bring a bag of ice over tomorrow," she volunteered. "You'll need it."

"Cool," Allie said.

"Of course it's cool—it's ice," Darcy joked.

Stephanie and Allie groaned at the same time.

Stephanie put away packages of matching plastic cups and plates. "You guys will have to help me bring my stereo downstairs. We've got the one in the family room, but we'll put mine in the kitchen."

"Wall-to-wall sound," Allie observed. "Excellent!"

Later, as she and her friends were sprawled on the living room floor, Stephanie heard D.J. let herself in. Stephanie looked up and saw her sister carrying an armload of books.

"Hi, D.J.," she called out. "We're planning my party. Could we ask you—" Stephanie stopped short. For some reason D.J. was wearing a pained expression on her face.

"Is something wrong?" Stephanie asked.

D.J. put down most of her books. She held on to one. "Well—yes, something's wrong," she admitted. "Could I talk to you for a minute up in your room?"

Stephanie hurried after her sister. *I wonder what happened,* she thought, feeling a flutter of alarm.

D.J. sat on the foot of Stephanie's bed. She said, "I'm really sorry about this, Steph, but you can't have your party."

Stephanie couldn't believe her ears. "What? Why not?"

D.J. held up the book in her hand. Stephanie saw the title was *Europe from Napoleon to World War II,* by Herman Overberg, Ph.D. "This is the reason," D.J. told Stephanie. "I'm really sorry."

"A college book? I don't understand." Stephanie felt tears fill her eyes.

D.J. sighed. "We're reading this in history. Dr. Overberg, the author, is in San Francisco for a conference. Tomorrow night he's agreed to hold a seminar for all the students taking history classes at college. My professor says we all have to go, so I can't be here to chaperone."

"Can't you get someone to take notes for you?" Stephanie wailed.

With a shake of her head, D.J. replied, "My professor says we have to be there. He's going to take attendance. I can't get out of it."

"But I've already invited—"

D.J. patted her shoulder. "I know. And I'm really sorry, Steph. I know how much your party means to you. If there were any other way, I'd say go for it. But there just isn't. Tomorrow you'll have to tell everyone that the party is canceled."

Stephanie couldn't answer.

This is terrible, she thought. *This is the end of my social life! People will think I'm so lame.*

Then an even worse thought came to her: *Bobby Michaels will think I'm lame. What am I going to do?*

MICHELLE

Chapter
3

Michelle opened the attic door and sneezed. Dust tickled her nose and made her eyes water. And it looked awfully dark in there.

She had led her best friends, Cassie Wilkins and Mandy Metz, upstairs, and she couldn't chicken out now. "I think there's probably a light somewhere," Michelle told her friends. She felt around on the rough wall and finally found a switch. When she flicked it, one weak bulb came on. It gave just enough light to make the shadows in the attic seem really dark.

The three girls crept inside. Michelle could

see that one small window let a little daylight leak in. But only a little. A stack of boxes blocked most of it.

"Do you see any spiders?" Cassie asked nervously. She crossed her arms as if trying to protect herself from a spider attack.

Mandy pointed. "I see some spider*webs*," she said. "And where there are spiderwebs, there must be spiders!" She stepped closer to Michelle and started to pat her hair as if afraid some creature were creeping around on her head.

"Come on," Michelle urged her friends. "Spiders won't hurt you. They're more afraid of you than you are of them."

"How can they be?" Cassie complained.

"What are we looking for?" Mandy wanted to know.

Michelle took a deep breath of warm, dusty air. "Some lights. They're like Christmas lights, but pink. They're up here somewhere. And we're looking for anything else that's fun."

"I don't see *anything* that looks like fun," Cassie said.

"Use your imagination," Michelle told her. "We're *exploring*."

She took a long look around. *Maybe it's a little creepy*, she thought, *but it's not that bad. And it will be fun to see what we can find up here!*

Out loud, she said, "Let's start searching. We're looking for anything new."

"New?" Mandy sounded surprised. "Nothing *new* would have this much dust on it!" Mandy leaned over a large dresser and blew. A cloud of dust rose off the surface.

"New to *us*, I mean," Michelle explained. "Look at this stuff. Some of the trunks look really old. There's no telling what might be in them!"

"Spiders," Cassie insisted.

"Maybe not," Michelle said. She bit her lip and thought for a minute. She wanted her friends to have fun. "Maybe there's a treasure up here," she suggested. She waggled her eyebrows. "It could be that a pirate was staying in San Francisco years and years ago. He could have left his treasure chest up here. Maybe he sailed off and forgot it. If we find it, it's all ours!"

"Right," Mandy said, but she didn't seem convinced. She rubbed her arms. "I'm starting to get creepy-crawly feelings."

"Let's start with these boxes that are close to the door," Michelle suggested. She was a little creeped out, too, but she was more curious than she was scared.

Michelle opened the first box. It didn't have the pink lights inside, but it *did* have a tightly packed bundle of clothes. They smelled like mothballs. Michelle gently unfolded a red velvet dress. "Look at this," she yelped. "It's from the olden days."

"Wow," Cassie said. "I'll say. This looks like it could have come from the 1970s."

Michelle squirmed into the dress. It was too long and *way* too big, but she held up the skirt and twirled around. "Disco city!" she cheered. "I wonder if I can find a hat. And maybe some shoes."

Mandy pulled out a man's dinner jacket. Once it might have been gleaming white. Now it was a dull yellowish-ivory color. Mandy tugged it on. It hung on her like a baggy tent. Still, Michelle thought it was kind of neat. Mandy spread out her arms and said, "Cool! I'd love to have this. I could roll up the sleeves."

Cassie dived in, too. She came up with a brown fake-fur jacket. She tried it on and asked, "How does it look?"

Michelle tilted her head. "You look like a movie star."

For a few minutes they dressed up in everything they could find. But then Michelle reminded herself, *We've got a job to do. We have to find those pink lights.*

"I'll ask Dad if we can have some of this stuff," she told her friends as she took off the dress. "Right now let's put everything away. We've got to hunt for party lights."

The next box was crammed with smaller boxes. One of these bulged with necklaces, bracelets, earrings, and other costume jewelry. Michelle found a long string of fake pearls. She looped it around her neck.

Mandy squealed with delight when she found a silver chain with a big round peace symbol dangling from it. And Cassie found a bracelet and necklace set. It looked like pale green jade, but Michelle thought it was probably plastic. Still, it was fun pretending they had found real treasure.

This is almost as good as finding a pirate treasure chest, she told herself. *Maybe I'll see if Steph likes any of this jewelry. She could wear it for the party.*

That thought reminded Michelle of the real reason they had come up to the attic. "Hey, guys," she said. "We still haven't found those lights." She pointed to a shadowy corner. "Let's look over there."

In that part of the attic, the slanted ceiling was so low, the girls had to duck to fit under it. Michelle spotted a small, square trunk. It was tucked far out of the way, in the darkest shadows of the attic. She grabbed its handle. Turning to her friends, Michelle said, "Help me pull this out. It looks *really* old."

It took a lot of pulling. At last the trunk slid away from the wall with a gritty, grinding sound. They hauled it to a clear space under the window. Cassie dusted her hands off and observed, "It's probably locked."

Michelle took a close look. "It doesn't even

have a lock," she pointed out. She pried at the rusty catch. Finally it squeaked open. The trunk lid groaned on dry hinges. Layers of crinkly brown paper lay inside. Under them Michelle found some strange little things: a bundle of dried daisies, a photo album with no pictures in it, and a small baby doll. Michelle lifted another layer of paper. She saw a little red book, maybe four by six inches. She fished it out and carried it to a place under the lightbulb.

Cassie peered over her shoulder. "What is it?"

Michelle tilted the book. On the red cover, the words "Daily Diary" were printed in faded gold letters. "Should we read it?" she asked.

"Are you *kidding?*" Mandy demanded. "Of course we should."

Michelle opened the diary. The handwriting wasn't very good, but it was clear enough. "I'll read it out loud," Michelle said.

She began: " 'September 15, 1953. Dear Diary, this is my eleventh birthday. My name is Erica. I have blond hair and blue eyes. I live in San Francisco with my dad, mom, and my fifteen-year-old sister, Jessica. I like horses and picnics by the ocean. I love long rides in the country. Once my family went to New York. I remember the Statue of Liberty. I was born in San Pedro. My dad works for a real estate company, and we moved to this house when I was a baby. I will be in the sixth grade this year. I will tell you all my secrets. Good night, dear Diary. I will write again tomorrow.' "

"Can you believe it?" Cassie exclaimed. "That diary is really old."

"I wonder where Erica is today," Mandy added. "She's probably ancient."

Michelle felt the same kind of excitement she heard in Cassie's and Mandy's voices. She had the weird feeling that Erica was speaking to her from the past. "She lived in *our* house," Michelle said as she read the next page. "She gives the address right here."

Cassie bent her neck so she could read the loopy handwriting. "I wonder if she went to our school."

"I don't think our school was *built* back then," Mandy put in.

"No, she didn't," Michelle couldn't help bouncing up and down with excitement. "Erica says here, she goes to Clairmont School. I don't think that school is even around today."

"Read some more," Mandy urged.

Michelle turned a few pages and read: " 'October 14, 1953. We are reading *Treasure Island* in class. It's about pirates and treasures. I like it, but there aren't any girls in it at all! Jim Hawkins is the hero. I think there should be a book about a girl having a pirate adventure. That would be so cool—' "

She's right, Michelle thought. *I agree with Erica!*

"They said *cool* back in the old days," Mandy blurted out. "I can't believe it. This is so . . . so cool!"

Michelle had stopped reading out loud. Her gaze continued down the page. She felt her eyes growing wide with surprise. "Omigosh!" she yelped. "You'll never believe this. Not in a million years."

"What?" Cassie demanded. "Tell me—what does it say?"

"Come with me," Michelle ordered. Her two friends followed as she climbed down out of the attic. They all raced downstairs.

"What's the rush? What did you find?" Mandy asked from behind Michelle.

"You'll find out!" Michelle shot back over her shoulder. "Let's go get Steph and D.J. I want them to hear this, too."

Michelle saw Stephanie at the front door. Steph's friends, Darcy and Allie, were just leaving. "What's up?" Stephanie asked dully as Michelle clattered to the bottom of the stairs.

"Come on," Michelle said. She found D.J. in the kitchen. Stephanie followed and sat in a chair, looking unhappy. Michelle held up the book and began, "You'll never guess—" She broke off when no one looked eager to hear her news. "Uh, is something wrong?"

"The party's off," Stephanie stated. "We can't have it."

"Why not?" Michelle asked.

"It's sort of my fault," D.J. explained. She quickly told Michelle and her friends about her college assignment.

"That's not fair," Cassie said. "Can't you talk to the principal or something?"

"Colleges don't have principals," Michelle told her.

D.J. shook her head. "There's no one to talk to. I have to go to the lecture, that's all. I can't be here to chaperone the party."

Michelle thought that Stephanie looked as if she were about to cry.

Steph said, "I'm stuck with *uninviting* everyone we asked to come. I'm going to look like an idiot."

Michelle slipped into the chair next to Stephanie. She hated to see her sister so disappointed. She held up the little red diary. "This will cheer you up. We found this in a trunk upstairs. It's been there for ages and ages. And it's got a big secret. Just listen!" Michelle opened the diary and read aloud again, " 'May 23, 1954: Dear Diary, I have some sad news. My dad got a new job in Palo Alto. He's decided that we have to move—' "

"I wonder what Palo Alto was like then," Cassie said. "Now it's filled with people who work with computers, like my cousin, Bob."

"That's not the important part," Michelle told her. "Listen to how the diary goes on: 'We have to move this summer. Dear Diary, I just had an idea. I'd like to leave something of myself here where I have had such great times. I will leave you, dear Diary. And you will be a clue to a treasure I will hide! It will be like *Treasure Island* in real life!' "

"Cool!" Mandy exclaimed. "Is there a map?"

"There's a clue!" Michelle replied. She held up the diary so everyone could see that Erica had written a poem.

It read:

There's something in storage,
Locked up tight,
In the place without a window of light.
If you can find it,
Then you will see,
A present there to you from me.

Michelle pointed to the page. "That's the last page Erica wrote on," she said. "Erica and her family must have moved right after she wrote it! And now I'm going to discover her treasure!"

Stephanie gave her a weak smile. "That's nice."

Michelle could tell that Steph felt bad. *She's thinking about the party*, Michelle realized. "It might be fun to hunt for the treasure," she told her sister. "You can help if you want."

Stephanie sighed. "I don't feel like it. But I hope you find it."

Michelle decided she could cheer up Stephanie later. Right now she had a treasure to hunt! She turned to D.J. "Can Mandy and Cassie help me search?"

D.J. smiled at her. "Sure. Have fun. Just try not to destroy the house."

"Let's go up to my room," Michelle said. Cassie and Mandy followed her up the stairs. When the three girls had settled on the bed, Michelle told them, "We have to figure out where this treasure is. And what it could be."

"Maybe it's a photograph of Erica," Mandy said. "It would be fun to see what she looked like."

"Or maybe it's a toy," Cassie suggested.

41

"The kind of toy they only made back in the fifties."

"I think the treasure is something much more mysterious," Michelle told them. She felt goosebumps on her arm whenever she thought about it. "I'll bet it's something totally amazing!"

Chapter
4

Well, Stephanie thought as the lunch bell rang on Friday, *at least it hasn't been too bad. Maybe I'm not going to be a social outcast after all!*

Allie and Darcy had been totally understanding about her problem. "Bummer, but that's the way it goes," Darcy had said with a shrug.

"Yeah," Allie agreed. "I guess the idea of a party without parents was too good to be true, anyway. I'm sorry, Steph."

Both Allie and Darcy had agreed to go around uninviting guests. Just before they split up to go to their classes that morning,

43

Stephanie had pleaded, "Guys, *please* smooth things over. Tell everyone that I'll reschedule the party for later."

"When?" Allie had wanted to know.

Feeling a little desperate, Stephanie had promised, "Soon. Really, really soon."

Allie and Darcy had gone to work. And that morning Stephanie uninvited half a dozen people herself. To her relief no one seemed too upset. Lots of kids seemed to have had a similar experience. Or at least lots of them seemed to understand her problem.

At lunch Steph learned from Allie and Darcy that just a few kids remained on the list to uninvite. "Okay, I'll see Kathy this afternoon," Allie said. "And Darcy can tell Jim and Paul. Oh, there's one person you'll have to tell, Steph. You have biology with Bobby Michaels, don't you?"

Yikes! Stephanie thought. *I have a hard time just trying to talk to him. How am I supposed to uninvite him to my party?*

She groaned and said, "I'll try to let him know this afternoon." It was not the kind of conversation she had daydreamed about having with Bobby. *Still*, she thought, *it's a start.* Sort of.

By the time Stephanie's afternoon biology class rolled around, everything else seemed under control. Stephanie and her lab partner, Chrissy, started their weekly experiment. Today they had to measure how much oxygen a gloppy green beaker of algae had produced since the week before.

Bobby was in the same lab. That made it hard for Stephanie to keep her mind on the algae, even though Bobby's lab table was all the way across the room. His lab partner was Donald Kincaid. Several times during lab, Stephanie caught them both looking at her. Once or twice Bobby gave her a friendly smile. Or did he?

Chrissy is standing right next to me, she realized. *Maybe it's Chrissy he's smiling at.*

The more Stephanie thought about having to uninvite Bobby, the less eager she felt to talk to him. *I don't know how to tell him*, she admitted to herself. *Not without making myself look very, very lame.*

For whatever reason, Stephanie didn't talk

much with Chrissy that day, even though they usually gabbed it up during lab. Was it because she felt a little twinge of jealousy about Chrissy and Bobby? Stephanie couldn't decide. She didn't want to be jealous of Chrissy.

When class was nearly over, Chrissy said, "I can deal with this kind of experiment. I just hope we don't have to cut up a dead frog." She began to store their lab equipment in the table drawer.

"That would be gross," Stephanie agreed, getting her books together. "I don't even like *live* frogs."

The bell rang, signaling the end of class.

"See you later," Chrissy said. She hurried away.

Better talk to Bobby, Stephanie told herself. *And I might as well get it over with.* But when she looked around, it was too late. Bobby had already ducked out the door. *Maybe I can ask someone else to tell him,* Stephanie thought with a feeling of relief.

Stephanie walked into the hall and headed for her next class. As she passed the school library, she heard someone call her name. She turned to see who it was.

"Stephanie!" It was Bobby! He shouldered his way through the crowd. Stephanie waited by a row of lockers as Bobby came up to her. He really was incredibly cute. Today he was wearing a sweater that was the exact same shade of green as his eyes.

He stood beside her, pressing himself against the wall. Students jostled past them. "Man, this place is like a can of sardines," he observed. "Live sardines." He glanced around. "So, uh, so what's up?"

"Not much," Stephanie said, smiling. *I can't just jump into telling him the party is off*, she realized. *I've got to be cool. Maybe I can lead up to the subject somehow.*

She thought of her favorite teen magazine, *Daisy*. It recommended starting a conversation with a boy by mentioning something you had in common. "So . . . how'd your algae do?" she asked.

"Huh?" Bobby blinked. "Oh, the algae. All right, I guess. It made some oxygen."

Stephanie cleared her throat. "That's what

it's supposed to do, all right." Her words sounded lame even to her. And somehow she couldn't help repeating them: "Yes, it's supposed to make that oxygen."

Bobby nodded. "Uh, yeah. Listen, I wanted to talk to you back in the lab. But you looked kinda busy with Chrissy. I know she's your lab partner, so . . ."

It was hard for Stephanie to keep the smile plastered on her face. It felt totally fake.

Chrissy! she thought. *Why does Bobby want to talk about her?*

Stephanie didn't want Bobby to know that she was feeling upset. She kept her voice under control. "Chrissy's been my lab partner from day one," she reported. "She's cool."

"I thought so," Bobby replied. Someone jostled him. He took a step sideways. "Hey, I also wanted to say that I'm looking forward to later."

Later? Stephanie realized he was talking about her canceled party. "Uh, Bobby, there's something I need to tell you—" she began.

The bell rang for the next class. "I'm gonna be late for math!" Bobby exclaimed. "Tell me whatever it is tonight. It'll be cool to have some time to hang out. See you." Bobby plunged back into the crowd. In a couple of seconds he had turned a corner and was out of sight.

"Umm, right," Stephanie agreed, talking to the spot where Bobby had been.

Bobby wants to hang out with me later, she thought. *Seriously awesome!*

But as she ran toward her next class, Stephanie realized that there wasn't going to be a "later," because there wasn't going to be a party. She had missed her chance to tell Bobby.

Stephanie wondered what she should do. *Bobby hasn't heard about the party. I should have told him it's canceled—but it's too late now.*

She ducked into her class just as the teacher started to call the roll. Whatever she did about the Bobby situation, she'd have to do it later.

I'll catch him after school, she told herself. *Or I'll call him. I just have to figure out what to say.* Stephanie thought hard, but her mind felt blank. Maybe if she wrote it out, she'd come up with a good way of explaining things.

Then she wouldn't be so nervous when they talked.

She began to write in her notebook, *Bobby, you know that party that I invited you to? The one that's supposed to be tonight? Well, I'm really sorry but I had to cancel—*

"Miss Tanner." Stephanie glanced up to see her English teacher glaring at her. "We haven't begun discussing classwork yet, so obviously you're not taking notes. Why don't you share whatever it is you're writing with the rest of the class?"

Stephanie felt her face turning bright red. *Great,* she thought. *Now I won't have to tell Bobby. My whole English class will do it for me.*

Chapter 5

A *present there to you from me,"* Michelle thought. *What could Erica's present be?* She was sitting in class. Her math book was open in front of her. For the last few minutes, though, Michelle had been lost in thought.

She couldn't wait to find the mysterious present that Erica had left for her. And she couldn't stop thinking about what it might turn out to be.

The hidden treasure could be almost anything. And it would be really, really old. It might even be valuable. Even if it wasn't worth much in money, the present was *sure* to

51

be something cool. Now, Michelle reasoned, her only problem would be finding it. To do that, she'd just have to figure out Erica's poem. . . .

"Michelle? Michelle, are you paying attention?" her teacher asked in a firm tone.

"Huh?" Michelle shook her head. "Oh, yes, I am." She held up her math book to prove it.

Her teacher smiled. "Then why don't you have your *English* book out? Math ended five minutes ago."

"Oops!" Michelle got her English book from her desk and hastily opened it. "Sorry."

"Page seventy-six," her teacher told her. "Now remember, a verb shows action or a state of being . . ."

Maybe I was daydreaming a little, Michelle realized. But it was so hard not to.

Only about half her mind thought about subjects and verbs. With the other half, Michelle was trying to imagine what Erica looked like. Maybe Erica loved jeans and sweatshirts. Or maybe she wore one of those cool poodle skirts.

Did Erica wear her hair in a ponytail? Did

she carry a backpack to school? A million questions buzzed in Michelle's mind. She couldn't wait to answer at least some of them by solving Erica's riddle and finding the treasure.

At recess she called Cassie and Mandy over to a corner of the playground. "Any ideas, you guys?" she asked. "I mean about where Erica could have hidden her surprise?"

Cassie shrugged. "Just what the poem says. It has to be somewhere without a window."

Mandy nodded. "So that's where we'll look. Everywhere in your house where there's no window. It's simple."

Michelle didn't feel satisfied with that. "But there are a *million* places without windows in our house. That could be inside or outside or anywhere."

"We can't do anything about it until after school, anyway," Mandy pointed out.

"And we're missing recess," Mandy added. "Come on. Let's play dodgeball." A loud, fast game was going on nearby. Kids were shrieking and leaping as they tried to dodge a big yellow plastic ball. It looked like fun.

"Okay," Michelle said.

They all ran over and joined the line. *Did Erica play dodgeball?* Michelle wondered. *Was that game even invented back in the fifties?*

Whap! The ball tagged her. Surprised, Michelle spun around. Mandy was grinning at her. "Gotcha!" she said. "You're supposed to *move*, Michelle."

There's a downside to daydreaming, Michelle realized. She promised herself that in the next round, when it was Mandy's turn, she was going to take especially good aim.

All day long Michelle felt the same. No matter what she was doing, she kept thinking about Erica and her hidden surprise. Possible answers to the riddle buzzed in her mind. "Locked up tight" made it sound as if the hidden treasure might be in a safe. Except the Tanners didn't have one.

"Storage" made her think of all the places her family kept things. But what about the "window of light?" And why was it so important that the hiding place didn't have one?

Michelle sighed. Cassie and Mandy were right. There was no way to solve the puzzle while she was in school. That would take some serious searching that she could only do at home. Michelle knew that she would just have to wait. But waiting was so hard.

That afternoon the class had art. Everyone was supposed to use crayons to sketch some people in an interesting place. Michelle drew a picture of a family of four.

"Cool," Karlee Johnson said when she looked at Michelle's drawing. "Is that supposed to be you, your dad, and your sisters?"

"No," Michelle told her. "This is a girl named Erica, and her sister and her mom and dad. They live in California. But in this picture, they're visiting New York." She pointed to a tall gray building that she had sketched in the background. "This is the Empire State Building."

"Very nice, Michelle," the teacher said, peering over Michelle's shoulder.

"I need some help," Michelle told her. "I want this picture to be in the 1950s. How can I make my drawing look old?"

Her teacher raised her eyebrows. "That's an interesting question. Maybe you can go to the media center and find a book about New York with some old photos in it. That might give you an idea about how to set your picture in that time."

Michelle did find a book like that. She leafed through it, staring at the old photos. After a few minutes she decided to put a yellow cab in her picture. She used a photo from the book for inspiration. Carefully Michelle drew in an old-fashioned car, with a rounded hood and rounded fenders.

"Very good work," her teacher said when she had finished. She looked at the big round clock above the chalkboard. "But now it's time for writing. Put away your pictures, and let's get out paper and pens."

Michelle practiced her handwriting. Today they were working on cursive *m*'s and *n*'s. While the class practiced, their teacher put the pictures the kids had drawn up on the bulletin boards around the room. Michelle kept glancing up at hers.

I don't know what they really looked like, but they could have looked just like that, Michelle told herself.

She stared at the picture. She wished the Erica in the drawing could talk. *Then she could give me a hint about where to look for her present*, Michelle thought.

But a crayon sketch couldn't do that. Michelle sighed. *Mandy, Cassie, and I will have to do it ourselves*, she decided.

Oh, well—when treasures were involved, finding them was at least half the fun!

Chapter
6

After school, Stephanie, Allie, and Darcy went to the Tanners' house for a soda. After all, there were plenty of sodas now. As they sat around the table, Stephanie told the others about talking to Bobby.

"He actually said he wanted to *hang out* with you?" Allie gushed. "Maybe that means he's got a crush on you."

"But I didn't get a chance to tell him the party was off!" Stephanie wailed. "I'd better call him, I guess."

Darcy waved down Stephanie's worries. "No biggie, Steph. Allie and I talked to almost everybody. So someone else probably told him, anyway."

"She's right," Allie put in. "I'm sure the word was spread. Even if nobody told Bobby by the time he went to bio, he's sure to have heard by the end of the day."

"You don't have to call him," Darcy agreed. "Hey, even if he shows up, we can just explain to him then, right?"

Stephanie sighed and nodded. "I guess," she said. "I'm probably worried about nothing. Still, just to be safe, maybe I'd better—"

Crash! Stephanie jumped up as a loud noise thundered from upstairs.

"Wow!" Allie said. "What was that?"

"It came from our room!" Stephanie exclaimed. "I'd better see what Michelle's doing." She ran up the stairs, with Allie and Darcy following.

Stephanie yanked open the door to their bedroom. Jeans, tops, skirts, and sweaters were spread all over the floor. And shoes! All of her shoes! She ducked as another pair flew out of her closet and banged on the floor. "Michelle! What's going on?" she yelled.

Michelle was on her hands and knees in Stephanie's closet. She backed out and said, "Hi, Steph. Want to help me?"

"Help you do what? Wreck the house?" Allie asked from the doorway.

"My clothes!" Stephanie wailed. "What are you doing with my clothes?"

Mandy and Cassie were on the same side of the room, burrowing into *Michelle's* closet.

"Don't worry, Steph," Michelle said. "We'll put all this stuff back as soon as we find it."

"It?" Darcy sounded confused. "What are you looking for?"

"We figure we'll know when we find it," Mandy explained.

"Whatever it is, it can't be sneakers," Cassie added, holding up a pair. "We already found a million of them!"

Stephanie flopped down on the cushioned window seat, exasperated. "All my stuff. Michelle, what's gotten into you?"

"We're looking for Erica's surprise," Michelle replied. "You know, the treasure the diary talked about."

Stephanie remembered the book and its

poem. "Oh, that. But the diary didn't say anything was hidden in my closet. Look at this
mess. Michelle, I don't mind you guys playing, but now my clothes are all wrinkled. And
my best sweaters are on the *floor*."

"We'll pick it all up," Michelle assured her.
"But we have to check out every closet in the
house."

Stephanie couldn't help rolling her eyes.
Didn't Michelle realize that everything in the
closets belonged to the Tanners? If there were
any treasures in the closets, someone in their
family would have noticed them before now.
She opened her mouth to say so, but the doorbell rang.

"Just leave the room the way you found it,
Michelle," Stephanie pleaded, and hurried
out to answer the door.

"What kind of treasure is it supposed to
be?" Allie asked as she and Darcy followed
Stephanie back downstairs.

"Who knows?" Stephanie answered. The
bell rang again. "Coming!" she yelled.

She opened the door and found a short,
balding man standing on their front porch. He

held something very, very long, wrapped in colored cellophane. "Miss Tanner?" he said with a smile. "I've got your sandwich."

Stephanie stood staring at the sandwich she had ordered the day before—all five feet of it. She had forgotten to cancel the order.

"Uh-oh," Allie said.

"That is a *big* sandwich," Darcy added.

Stephanie took a deep breath. "Uh, we don't need it now," she said. "Could you take it back?"

The man shook his head. "Sorry, Miss Tanner. Once a sandwich is made, it's sold. I can't take it back."

Stephanie sighed. "I was afraid you'd say that. Wait here. I'll get the money." She turned to her friends. "Allie, Darce, would you take the sandwich to the kitchen? And please, please, *please*—promise me you'll stay for dinner."

Later that evening Stephanie, Allie, and Darcy sprawled out in the living room, watching TV. Stephanie stifled a large burp. "We're never going to eat the whole thing," she said. More than four feet of sandwich remained.

Darcy groaned. "Doesn't Michelle want any?"

"She doesn't like hero sandwiches," Stephanie replied. "And neither do her friends. They fixed themselves some peanut butter and jelly—"

The phone rang. Stephanie, feeling stuffed to the gills, pushed herself up to answer it. "Hello, Tanner residence."

"Hi, Steph." Danny's voice reached her through the receiver. "How's everything?"

"Oh, hey, Dad. Everything here is fine," Stephanie said.

"Great," Danny replied. "Put D.J. on, please."

"She's not home," Stephanie reported. She explained about D.J.'s seminar.

"She left you and Michelle there *alone*?" Danny sounded alarmed.

"We're not alone," Stephanie said patiently. "Allie and Darcy are here, and Michelle has a couple of friends over. Anyway, it's no big deal. D.J. said she'd be back home before Michelle's bedtime."

"I could get a flight home—" Danny began.

Stephanie laughed. "Dad, I love you, but you worry too much. We'll be okay. Really. Come back on Sunday, just like you planned."

After a little more convincing on Stephanie's part, Danny decided to do just that. Then he gave Stephanie a few more minutes of what Allie called "dadly advice" before saying good-bye. Stephanie hung up. "Anyone want a little more of the sandwich?" she asked without much hope.

Allie and Darcy whimpered. Stephanie flopped back onto the sofa. "So what's on TV?"

"One of those funny home video shows," Darcy told her.

"Let's see if there's anything else on—" Stephanie said. The doorbell cut her off.

Allie looked alarmed. "Don't tell me you ordered more food. Please say you didn't."

Stephanie shook her head and got up again. "Maybe D.J. got back early and forgot her key or something," she said.

When she opened the door her jaw

dropped. *Bobby Michaels* was standing in front of her, along with three other kids from school—Freddie Packard, Lana Yardley, and Daphne Coleman.

"Hi," Bobby said with his brilliant smile. He looked great in dark jeans, a black T-shirt, and a gray fleece vest. "I guess we're a little early, huh?"

Stephanie felt her heart thud with panic. *Oh, no! Bobby didn't get the word about the party!*

"R-right," she stammered. "You're early. *Way* early."

"Oh! But Allie and Darcy are here so I guess the party's started," Bobby observed. He stepped into the living room. "Come on in, guys." He motioned to the three other kids. They all trooped in and took seats in the living room.

Stephanie stared pointedly at Allie and Darcy. They shook their heads.

Four kids, Stephanie thought. *It's only four kids. Four kids is not a party. It's just hanging out.*

There's nothing wrong with hanging out, Stephanie reasoned. *And Bobby's right. It's early. D.J. won't be home for at least three hours!*

Then she thought of something else: the sandwich!

Well, there was nothing wrong with having six friends over to hang out and eat sandwiches for a couple of hours.

What could *possibly* go wrong?

Chapter
7

Whew!" Michelle said. She closed the door of her dad's closet. "Dad sure had a lot of stuff in there."

"Tell me about it," Mandy agreed. "And now there's a lot of his stuff out here. *Everything's* out here, in fact!"

Michelle surveyed the damage. Well, maybe *damage* wasn't the right word. *Mess* was closer. Even though they'd tried really hard to be neat.

Mandy, Cassie, and Michelle had started laying out all of Danny's suits on the bed, but some had sort of slipped to the floor. And

6 7

Danny had almost as many shoes as Michelle and Stephanie had sneakers. He was fussy about them, too. He kept everything super-neat and in a special order.

"We'll have to pair up all the shoes," Michelle told her friends. "If we don't, Dad will know we were messing around in his closet."

"Do we have to put them back now?" Cassie objected. "We haven't found Erica's surprise yet."

Michelle tried not to think about all the closets they had emptied—there were a lot of them. Which meant there was a lot to clean up.

Then again, her father wouldn't be home for a while.

"No. We don't have to do it right away," Michelle decided. "We can clean up later— after we find Erica's surprise."

"Okay," Cassie said. "Where do we look next?"

Michelle sat on the foot of her dad's bed. She rested her chin on her hand and thought. "Hmmm. I was sure it would be in a closet.

'Something in storage, locked up tight, in the place without a window of light.' "

"We've been through all the closets upstairs," Mandy pointed out.

"It couldn't be in the attic," Cassie added. "That has a window, and a little light comes through it."

" 'In storage,' " murmured Michelle. "Where else, besides closets, do you store stuff? It has to be in the house somewhere."

Mandy scratched her nose. "My mom keeps some stuff in a wall safe."

"We don't have a wall safe," Michelle said. Then she got a sudden idea. She hopped off the bed. "Come on. I've got it! I know just the place that Erica must have meant."

"Cool!" Cassie exclaimed. "Uh—where?"

"There's a storage space under the stairs! Uncle Joey keeps stuff in there!" Michelle opened the bedroom door and winced. Music pounded up from downstairs. Loud music. "What's going on down there?" she wondered.

Michelle started down the stairs, but she stopped halfway down. She couldn't believe what she saw. A dozen or more kids were dancing in the living room! And the stereo was cranked up so high, the windows were rattling.

Cassie said something, but Michelle couldn't hear. She shook her head. Cassie leaned closer and bellowed, "What's happening?"

"It looks a lot like a party," Michelle yelled back. "D.J.'s not gonna like this." She checked out the party scene. Stephanie was talking to a girl with short, blond hair. Darcy and Allie were dancing. It looked like fun, but Michelle had more important things to do. "Come on!" she shouted.

Michelle led Mandy and Cassie to the small door that opened into the storage space. She tried to pull it open. The door was stuck. Michelle gave it a few strong tugs.

"Got it," Michelle said as the door jerked open. She and her friends peered into the storage space.

"Wow!" Cassie said. "Joey sure has a lot of junk."

"Tons of it," Mandy added.

"Well, we have to go through all of it," Michelle decided. "We've got to be totally thorough."

She and her friends burrowed in. They started checking out every item in the storage area. Some of it was just ordinary stuff, like tennis racquets with broken strings. There were also things that Joey used in his comedy acts. Michelle saw a ventriloquist dummy. Cassie found a stage makeup kit crammed with false beards and rubber noses. Mandy dug up part of a clown outfit, one with big floppy red shoes and a belt with a bicycle horn on it.

None of that was what they were looking for. They tossed everything out behind them, into the noisy living room. As they cleared the space, Michelle, Mandy, and Cassie crept farther inside.

The spot under the stairs was small. The stairs made a kind of zigzaggy slanting ceiling in the space. Joey had put a rod across the tallest side and hung old clothes and costumes there. Michelle, Cassie, and Mandy took them down.

"Michelle!" Stephanie's voice called. Michelle looked around. Her older sister was peering in the doorway. "What are you doing?"

"Looking for the treasure," Michelle explained again.

"This is Uncle Joey's stuff!" Stephanie yelled.

"We'll put it back!" Michelle shouted over the thumping bass of a CD.

"Why are you making such a mess? And don't you know you're not allowed in there? You have to stop searching right now!" Stephanie ordered.

"Don't you know *you're* not supposed to have this party?" Michelle shot back.

"This *isn't* a party!" Stephanie insisted. "It's just—just some hanging out that got out of hand!"

The song ended, and in the short silence Michelle heard the phone ringing. "Better get it," she said. "That could be Dad."

"Oh, no!" Stephanie exclaimed.

"I'll get it." Michelle wriggled out of the storage space. She ran to the phone and picked it up. The stereo fired up again. "Hello!" Michelle yelled into the receiver.

"Michelle?" It *was* Danny. Michelle clapped her hand over her free ear so she could hear him. "I just called to see if D.J. has checked in."

"Uh, she's coming home later," Michelle yelled. The CD player roared with the sounds of guitars and a bass drum. "Steph and I are okay, though."

"What's that loud music I hear?" Danny demanded.

"The music?" Michelle shouted. She looked up into Stephanie's pleading face. *She could really get in trouble,* Michelle thought. Very loudly, she said to Danny, "It's nothing. Stephanie is just playing a new CD."

"Tell her to turn it down," Danny advised. "You don't want to bother the neighbors. Or wake up the dead."

"Okay, got it," Michelle said. "I'll have D.J. call you when she gets in, all right?"

"Good idea," Danny said. "Love you. Tell Stephanie to turn that CD player down!"

"Okay, bye." Michelle hung up the phone. She turned to Stephanie and said, "You owe me big time."

Stephanie gave her a weak smile. "Have fun hunting for your treasure."

"Thanks! And Dad says to turn the music down!" Michelle looked around. Even more kids seemed to have shown up. *Maybe loud music attracts teenagers*, Michelle thought. *Sort of like lights attract moths.* She could see that Steph was going to have to fight her way over to the stereo.

Michelle dived back into the storage space. Cassie and Mandy had pretty much emptied everything out. Now the spot under the stairs was bare. "No luck," Cassie reported.

"Maybe it's behind a secret panel or something," Mandy suggested.

Michelle brightened. "I'll bet that's it. A secret compartment! Knock on the floors and walls. We'll find it."

They began to tap. Then someone walked past the storage-space door and gave it a hard shove. It slammed behind them. Suddenly Michelle, Mandy, and Cassie were in total darkness!

Michelle felt her way to the door. She fumbled around and found the handle. She gave it a twist, but it didn't move.

"Open the door," Cassie said. "It's dark in here."

"I'm trying," Michelle told her. "The door's a little stuck."

"A little *stuck*?" Mandy echoed. "What do you mean?" She sounded nervous.

"Just a second." Michelle rattled the handle, but it wouldn't turn. She shoved at the door. It didn't budge.

"I don't like this," Mandy said. "It's stuffy in here."

Michelle banged on the door. "Hey!" she yelled. "Let us out."

Loud music pounded outside. No one could hear her. She couldn't compete with the drummer on the CD.

"Help!" Cassie shouted. Still no answer.

"Let's all try it together," Michelle suggested. "On three. One, two, three—*Helllp!*"

The three of them yelled as loudly as they could. But thanks to the music and dancing, no one in the living room could hear them.

They were trapped—trapped together in the small, dark space.

Chapter 8

Stephanie turned down the volume on the stereo—just as her dad had asked. A few seconds later, though, someone turned it up again.

Oh, well, Stephanie thought. *Might as well go with the flow.* Allie and Darcy were dancing nearby in the middle of a crowd of kids. Stephanie bopped her way over and motioned them into the foyer. It was a little quieter there.

"You guys, how many people are *here*?" Stephanie asked.

"Gee, just about everybody," Allie told her.

"I saw some kids using the phone. I guess they called everyone at school and told them the party was on, after all. So everybody we *un*invited, got *re*-invited. And they all showed up!"

Stephanie gulped. "That's, like, thirty people!"

"Yeah, isn't it awesome?" Darcy asked. "Plus, everyone's eating the sandwich. It's more than half gone. There's maybe only two feet left."

The sandwich is the least of my worries, Stephanie thought, as she surveyed the crowd of bodies moving to the beat.

Her eyes suddenly widened in alarm as she recognized two faces. "Oh, no!" she moaned. "Who invited *them*? And who let them in?"

Mark Arnett and Steven Pascoe, trouble-makers extraordinaire, were dancing over by the sofa. Actually, Steven Pascoe was dancing *on* the sofa.

Allie winced. "Yikes! He's using your couch as a trampoline," she said. "Something tells me your dad would not approve."

"No kidding. This has got to stop,"

Stephanie said in alarm. She started toward Steven Pascoe. But before she reached the sofa, the song ended. Steven stopped bouncing on the furniture and sat down to talk to Daphne Coleman instead.

Which reminded Stephanie: Daphne still arrived with Bobby. And she hadn't seen Bobby since he first got there.

Stephanie turned around to find that Allie and Darcy were right behind her. "Did either of you see Bobby?" she asked. Her two friends exchanged a glance.

"Should we tell her?" Allie asked.

"Tell me what?" Stephanie demanded.

"Well, Bobby's probably in the kitchen," Darcy said in a reluctant voice. "He's, uh, he's been hanging out in there with Chrissy since she got here."

Stephanie's heart felt heavy. *Maybe I just imagined that he was interested in me*, she thought. *Or maybe he just thought my party would be a good place to talk to Chrissy!*

"Are you okay?" Allie asked.

Stephanie nodded. "Yeah. I'm fine."

Darcy gave her an encouraging little push.

"Then find Bobby and talk to him," she suggested.

"Forget the kitchen," Allie said, pulling Stephanie back. "They're over there. By the bookshelves."

Stephanie had to stand on tiptoe to see across the crowded living room. She winced as she caught sight of Bobby. He was still with Chrissy!

What if I go talk to him, and he brushes me off? Stephanie worried. *What if he really likes Chrissy and thinks I'm just bothering him?*

But then she took a deep breath. *Get a grip,* Stephanie told herself. *Go for it. Chrissy's not bad. In fact, she's my friend. And if Bobby likes her, well, that's no reason for me not to talk to him—or to feel jealous!*

She wove her way across the crowded room. Bobby and Chrissy stood side by side against the far wall. "Great party!" Bobby yelled over the music as Stephanie neared them.

"Uh, thanks," Stephanie replied. "Um, are you guys having an okay time and all?"

Chrissy nudged Bobby, and he turned toward her. They gave each other a smile. It was the kind of smile you gave someone who shared a secret with you.

Whoa, Stephanie thought. *What's going on here? Am I interrupting something private?*

"We're having a great time, Steph," Chrissy said. "The food's amazing—"

The phone rang.

"Hold that thought," Stephanie said. She raced to the kitchen.

She edged around a crowd of boys who were chowing down on chips and dip. Then she stepped over Comet. She lunged for the phone. "Tanner residence."

"Hi, Steph." It was D.J. "We're at a break in the seminar. You guys doing okay?"

"Umm, fine," Stephanie told her.

"I'm going to stop at the store on the way home to get a lightbulb for the front porch," D.J. went on. "Is there anything you want?"

"No. I think we've got everything," Stephanie told her. From the corner of her eye, she watched Comet con one of the boys into giving him a potato chip.

"All right. I'll be home in, oh, two hours or so . . ." D.J. paused. "Hey, what's that music?"

Stephanie swallowed hard. "Uh, Allie and Darcy are here. They're playing a new CD that Allie bought."

"That's good. Maybe they'll help you forget about missing the party," D.J. went on. "Anyway, as long as I'm making a stop, check and see if Michelle wants anything, will you?"

"Sure, hold on." Stephanie punched the HOLD button. She took the cordless phone into the living room. Her friends—along with some kids she didn't know—were dancing like maniacs. Mark Arnett was juggling empty soda cans. No Michelle anywhere.

Stephanie headed for the stairs. Several couples sat on them, shouting over the music. Stephanie stepped around them and made her way upstairs. Nope. Michelle wasn't in their bedroom, either. Where could she be?

Stephanie closed the door to their bedroom, shutting out the noise from downstairs.

She grabbed the upstairs extension and hit the HOLD button. "Uh, D.J.? I think Michelle's up in the attic somewhere. You told her she could look for that treasure she read about in the diary, remember? She's kind of, um, busy right now."

"Oh, right," D.J. said. "Well, I'll try to find some little surprise for her at the store."

"I'm sure whatever you pick up will be fine," Stephanie assured her. Whew! It was a good thing D.J. wasn't insisting she find Michelle at that moment.

"Okay, seminar's about to start again. See you in two hours, Steph!"

Stephanie switched off the phone. *Great,* she thought. *It's not enough that I have to worry about an out-of-control party. And Bobby and Chrissy. And Mark Arnett and Steven Pascoe. Now I've got to find Michelle!*

Stephanie went to the attic stairs and yelled, "Michelle? Are you up there?" When she didn't get an answer, she headed back toward the living room and met Darcy on the stairs. "Have you seen Michelle and her friends?" she asked.

Darcy shook her head. "Not lately. Right now I just hope they're not in your bathroom, because that's where I'm going!"

Stephanie checked out the ground floor and

didn't see Michelle. When Darcy came back downstairs, Stephanie took her aside. "I can't find Michelle," she said. "I'm getting kind of worried. Will you help me look for her?"

"No problem," Darcy assured her. "The party's fun, but I think I'm going a little deaf from the volume."

Stephanie and Darcy began to search the house. Stephanie groaned when they opened the door to D.J.'s room. Her clothes had all been taken out of her closet, too. And their dad's room was even worse. Danny could tell if a lamp had been moved a quarter of an inch. What would he say when he got back and found that his closet had been ransacked?

They went up to Uncle Jesse and Aunt Becky's apartment.

"Terrific," Stephanie said. "The human tornadoes have ripped through here, too."

"Maybe they're in the other part of the attic," Darcy suggested.

"I yelled and they didn't answer," Stephanie replied. "Let's check, though." They went in and clicked on the single light. There was no one in sight.

"How about trying the basement?" Darcy suggested.

It was worth a shot, Stephanie thought. They clambered back down the stairs, and Allie came over to join them. Stephanie explained the problem. "I'll help you search," Allie volunteered.

They made their way toward the basement stairs. More and more kids were dancing, so it was a little like running an obstacle course. And someone had put on another CD, this one twice as loud as the others.

On the good side, though, Stephanie didn't see either Steven Pascoe or Mark Arnett. *Maybe they left,* she thought with relief.

Joey's apartment was in the basement. Stephanie opened his door and did a quick search. The girls weren't there.

"That leaves the other part of the basement," she told her friends.

The rest of the basement was just storage space, dark and empty. "Michelle?" Stephanie called. "Are you down here?"

Stephanie was beginning to feel seriously creeped out. Something cold touched her hand! Stephanie yelped and jumped a mile. She spun around—

"Comet!" she said in relief. The dog nudged her again with his cold, wet nose. "Where's Michelle?" Stephanie asked.

The dog wasn't talking.

Overhead the ceiling vibrated from music and dancing. Allie winced. "Maybe they went outside to get away from the music," she suggested.

"Or maybe they're out there treasure hunting," Darcy added.

Stephanie had a sudden vision of Michelle and her two friends ripping up the lawn with picks and shovels. "Come on," she said. "Let's check."

Outside, the neighborhood was quiet, as usual. Except that the Tanner house was thumping like a jukebox. Luckily, the neighbors on both sides seemed to be away for the evening. At least, their windows were dark.

Stephanie, Allie, and Darcy went back inside through the front door. They found an empty spot on the stairs and sat down. Stephanie's head whirled with a million worries. How could she lose her little sister? Especially in her own house?

"I don't get it," Stephanie yelled over the pulsing beat of the stereo. "Would she have gone over to Cassie's or Mandy's without telling me?"

"It's possible," Darcy shouted. "She's just a kid!"

"But she never does things like that," Stephanie objected.

"You never throw a party like this one," Allie pointed out. "It's an unusual night all around."

Stephanie made a face. "Well, I'm worried!"

"Where did you see her last?" Darcy asked.

Stephanie thought for a second. "Over there, on the phone." Then Stephanie remembered the cordless kitchen phone in her hand. She had been carrying it around with her. "Come on," she said. She made her way back to the kitchen to put the phone on its cradle.

Stephanie's breath caught in her throat when she pushed through the swinging door to the kitchen.

The crowd there had vanished. But Stephanie could tell that Mark and Steven had definitely been there. Salsa was splattered on one wall, onion dip on another. A puddle of cola dripped down the front of the stove. Empty cookie boxes and ice cream containers littered the table. Broken potato chips were everywhere.

"Oh, man," Darcy said. "What a mess!"

Stephanie gulped. She felt sick to her stomach. "I can't deal with that now," she said. "I've got to find Michelle first."

"Maybe you'd better call Cassie's mom and check with her," Allie suggested. "And if they're not there, check with Mandy's folks."

Stephanie shook her head. "Not yet. Right now, I'm the only one who's worried. If I start calling, I'm going to upset everyone. I just need a few minutes to think of places where they could be."

They threaded their way back through the dancing couples in the living room and sat on the stairs again. Stephanie hugged her knees. She wished she'd never even *thought* of throwing a party.

The song on the CD player ended. "We've got to find them," Stephanie said. "I wonder if—"

"Mrrph!" A sound met Stephanie's ears. She glanced at her friends.

Allie and Darcy looked at each other, then at Stephanie. "What?" they both asked at the same time.

"Did one of you say something?" Stephanie asked them.

"We thought you did," Allie told her.

The music was playing again. Stephanie stood up and yelled, "Hey, guys, turn off the stereo for a second, okay?"

Mark Arnett switched it off. "Great party!" he exclaimed, giving Stephanie a thumbs-up.

"Yeah. Thanks," Stephanie said, trying to smile. "We're looking for my little sister. Has anyone seen Michelle?"

"Mrrrrrffffffffffphhhhh!"

Darcy jumped up. "That came from under us!"

Stephanie felt a wave of relief. "I don't believe it." She pushed her way back to the storage-area door. Now that the music was off, Stephanie could hear a steady thumping from the other side of the door.

Well, she thought, *D.J. may kill me for having this party, and Dad may kill me for letting my sister and her friends mess around in his closet, but at least one thing went right tonight.*

I finally found Michelle!

Chapter 9

Michelle was feeling hot. The storage space under the stairs was meant to hold *things*—not *people*! Especially not *three* people. Michelle and her friends were wedged in so tightly that Cassie's elbow pressed against Michelle's ribs. The air smelled dusty and stale. Everything felt muggy and damp. Worst of all, though, it was dark. No light leaked in, not even around the door.

"Come on," Michelle urged her two friends. "One more time. We've got to push it open."

"We've tried," Cassie complained. "We

can't do it, Michelle. There's not enough room for us to really move. Besides, the door is stuck too hard."

"Then we have to unstick it!" Michelle declared. "Come on. One really good push might do it. Unless you want to spend the rest of your lives in here."

"Okay, okay," Mandy said. "Let's all push together."

"Ready?" Michelle asked. She tensed her muscles. "Okay. One! Two! *Three!*"

The shove that Michelle, Cassie, and Mandy gave the door *might* have opened it.

It might have—if someone hadn't suddenly pulled on the door from the outside.

The door groaned open. Cassie, Mandy, and Michelle were all off balance. Their heads and shoulders tumbled out of the storage space. Michelle found herself facedown, with someone heavy lying on her back. "Get off me!" she mumbled.

"Sorry," Cassie said. She rolled off Michelle.

Michelle pushed herself up. She heard Darcy giggling like crazy. Other older kids started to laugh, too. They were standing around in a circle. Everyone was staring at Michelle and her friends.

"I'm sorry, Michelle," Darcy said. "You three just looked so funny, popping out of that little door."

"You're not hurt, are you?" Stephanie asked.

Michelle shook her head. Then she noticed how quiet everything was—she couldn't hear anything but snickering.

Great, Michelle thought, feeling her cheeks turn hot with embarrassment. *Now I've done it. They even switched off the music to laugh at us!*

Stephanie stood in front of her, a stern look on her face. "Michelle? Are you hurt?" she repeated.

"No, I'm fine," Michelle said, trying to smile. "Uh, hi." She gave her sister a little wave.

Stephanie shook her head slowly, as if she couldn't believe what had just happened. "How in the world did you get stuck in there?"

"Uh, see, this was the last closet in the house that we hadn't explored and we were—" Michelle began.

Stephanie held up a hand. "You were looking for that hidden surprise. I know. Don't even try to explain," she told her sister. "I've got too much to worry about right now."

Michelle blinked. "Okay." What a relief. She didn't have to explain. This party was a totally lucky break.

"Come on," Stephanie said to Darcy and Allie. "D.J. will be home soon. We've got to tell everyone . . ."

Someone cranked the stereo up again. Full blast. The music rattled the windows. In a moment all of Stephanie's guests began dancing again.

Michelle motioned to her friends to follow her. They went out onto the dark front porch. It was cooler there. And quieter.

Michelle took deep gulps of refreshing air. It smelled great, especially after the stale air under the stairs. She sat on the edge of the porch, and her two friends sat on either side of her.

"Well, that was . . . dusty," Cassie said. She slapped her hands over her clothes. "So was the attic." She sneezed. "And so's my nose!" She sneezed again.

"Maybe that was Erica's surprise," Mandy suggested. "Maybe she hid historic dust for us to find."

Cassie sneezed again. "In that case, I think I've found enough."

Michelle put her elbows on her knees and rested her chin in both hands. She closed her eyes to concentrate. "We've ruled out lots of places. The treasure has to be somewhere else," she said slowly. "So where do we look next?"

Mandy gasped. "What!"

"Are you kidding?" Cassie demanded. "You want to keep looking?"

"We've dug through every closet in your house," Mandy pointed out. "We've made a mess that will take a *year* to clean up. And we just got locked up in a place where nobody might have found us for days."

"My dad would have found us on Sunday," Michelle told her.

"Oh, that would have been great," Cassie said. "By Sunday, we'd be totally starved!"

"But nothing bad happened," Michelle reminded her. "Nothing really bad, anyway.

As soon as she heard us, Stephanie let us out. And nobody's hurt, right?"

"Right," Mandy and Cassie agreed.

"Then where do we look next?" Michelle asked again. "Come on, guys. This search isn't just playing around, you know. A treasure hunt is an adventure! And when you're on an adventure, you have to *expect* some excitement."

"I wasn't excited," Cassie grumbled. "Just hot. And dusty."

"But it *was* kinda fun trying to break out," Mandy said. "And at least we gave everyone a good laugh."

"Come on, Cassie," Michelle said. "We're fine, and we're getting closer to the treasure. Look at all the places we've been. We know it isn't in any of them, so we've narrowed down the search. I know—let's look in the basement."

The three of them trooped back inside and down the stairs. Joey's apartment took up half the basement. But his closet was a disappointment. So was the basement storage space. All it held was some old furniture and some skis that Danny used once in a while.

"Do you still think we're getting closer?" Cassie asked after twenty minutes of searching.

"Sure," Michelle replied. "We're *still* narrowing it down." They went back upstairs and found the kitchen crowded. And the living room was still jammed and noisy. Michelle led her two friends back out to the front porch. They sat down on the edge again. "Let's think," Michelle urged. "We need a clue."

"We *have* a clue," Mandy reminded the other two. "It has to be someplace without a window."

"So let's think of all the places without windows," Michelle suggested. "Places we haven't looked yet."

"Hmmm . . . the shower?" Mandy asked.

"But you couldn't *hide* anything in a shower," Cassie objected. "Unless you put it down the drain or in the showerhead."

Michelle considered that. "You know—"

Mandy cut her off quickly. "Stop right there. I don't think your dad would like us playing plumber, Michelle."

Cassie wrinkled her forehead. "How about, uh . . . the kitchen cabinets?" she asked.

"I don't think so," Michelle said slowly. "With a family like ours, someone looks in them every day. If Erica left her treasure in a kitchen cabinet, someone would have found it a long time ago."

"Under the refrigerator?" Mandy offered.

"No good," Michelle replied. "The refrigerator's not all that old. I remember when Dad bought it. So Erica's surprise would have been found when they moved the old refrigerator out."

For a few minutes none of them came up with anything. "I'm ready to give up," Cassie announced.

Michelle sighed. *Why did Erica make it so hard?* she wondered. *This treasure hunt is starting to look hopeless!*

Michelle wasn't the kind of girl who gave up easily, though. "There *has* to be another place we haven't searched," she insisted. "If we could just think of it."

Cassie yawned. "I'm starting to hate looking for stuff," she murmured. "You know what really bugs me? Losing the TV remote. It's always the last place you look. And it's usually right under your nose."

"Under your nose!" Michelle yelled. "That's it!"

"Huh?" both of her friends said together.

"Under your nose," Michelle repeated. "Cassie, you're *brilliant*."

"I am?" Cassie asked.

"Yes!" Michelle told her. "There *is* one place we haven't looked. A place with no windows. A place that's part of the house. And right now, it's under our noses!"

"I don't get it," Mandy complained.

Michelle was almost jumping up and down with excitement. "Well, not just under our noses, but under *us*! There's a storage space under this front porch. That's where the old lawnmower and some yard tools are kept. That has to be it. That has to be the place where Erica hid her treasure!"

Chapter 10

All right, here's the plan," Stephanie said to Darcy and Allie, her voice like a drill sergeant's. "We've got just one hour before D.J. will be home. You two suggest to everyone that it might be a good idea to wind down. Ask our friends to spread the word. Alice and Stan will help. Then maybe if a few kids start to leave, the others will get the message."

"Just throw everyone out," Darcy suggested. "Tell them D.J.'s on her way home and they've got to go."

"I can't," Stephanie told her. "I don't want

99

everyone to think I didn't plan to have this party. It would look totally uncool."

"Okay," Allie agreed. "But what about you? While we're roaming around doing that, what are you going to do?"

"Well—" In spite of everything, Stephanie couldn't help smiling. "Well, for one thing, I'll talk to Bobby. He's in the student government and all. So maybe he can use his leadership talents to persuade people—especially Mark Arnett and Steven Pascoe—to leave, you know?"

Darcy laughed. "Oh, sure, *we* know." She looked past Stephanie and nudged her. "And now's your chance. Bobby's standing right over there. He's still talking to Chrissy."

Stephanie turned. Bobby had one hand against the wall. He was leaning close and talking to Chrissy.

Stephanie squared her shoulders. "I'll just have to interrupt them," she declared.

"Go get 'em, Steph," Allie urged.

"We'll talk your guests into leaving," Darcy added. "Don't worry."

Stephanie weaved her way through the

dancing couples again. Chrissy threw back her head and laughed at something Bobby said. Then she seemed to notice Stephanie. Chrissy said something to Bobby. He pushed away from the wall and smiled at Stephanie.

Keep it casual, Stephanie told herself. *Chrissy's still your friend. If she likes Bobby, and Bobby likes her—well, you can deal. Nobody's out to hurt you on purpose. Just play it casual and cool.* Out loud, she said, "Sooo, have you guys had a good time?"

"Well, actually," Chrissy said with one quick glance at Bobby, "I was just telling Bobby that I'm hungry. So I'm going to see if I can track down what's left of that monster sandwich. See you two later." She gave Bobby a wink and walked away.

Stephanie felt her heart sink. The wink seemed to say everything. Now that she had her chance to talk to Bobby, she couldn't think of how to begin. For a second she stood there speechless. Then she forced some words out, though they didn't seem to pass through her brain on the way. "Uh, hope you, uh, enjoyed the music. And everything," she mumbled, immediately feeling foolish.

He'll think I'm fishing for compliments. She scolded herself. *And what is he going to say? "No, I had a terrible time?"*

But Bobby didn't seem to pick up on her awkwardness at all. "Oh, yeah, your party was cool," he said. "I've had a great time. I'd like to stay longer, but I'd better get home. This weekend I have a book report to do, and my folks want me to mow the lawn tomorrow, and—well, I'd better be leaving."

Leaving with Chrissy, I'll bet, Stephanie thought. But she forced herself to smile. "Okay. It's time the party ended, anyway. Maybe you could sort of let people know that? Especially people like Mark and Steven. It would help a lot. Anyway, I'm glad you could stop by."

"Do you know where my jacket is?" Bobby asked, looking around. "Darcy took it when I got here, but I don't know where she put it."

Stephanie remembered seeing a big pile of jackets and sweaters on the foot of her bed—a pile that Michelle and her friends *hadn't* thrown out of her closet. "She probably tossed it upstairs," she said. "I'll go find it for you and meet you by the front door."

"Thanks. You know what it looks like?" Bobby asked.

"Yeah, I know. I'll just be a second," Stephanie assured him.

She hurried upstairs. Bobby had been among the first to arrive, so she burrowed to the bottom of the stack and quickly found his gray fleece vest. *I just can't believe it*, she thought as she pulled it out. *Here I am at this big party I'm not even supposed to be having, and all the party has done is give Bobby a chance to hang out with the person he really likes—Chrissy! I feel so dumb.*

As Stephanie turned, clutching Bobby's jacket, a couple of girls came to the doorway. "We had a good time," one of them said with a smile. "But Faith and I have to leave, so we came to get our sweaters."

"Great music," the other one agreed. "Thanks a lot for having us over."

"Uh—glad you enjoyed it." Stephanie frowned, wondering who they were. She didn't even recognize them. *There really were a lot of people here,* she realized.

Holding Bobby's jacket, she hurried downstairs. Darcy and Allie must have been doing their jobs well. A dozen kids told her they had enjoyed themselves—and they were leaving. A steady stream went out the front door into the darkness.

Bobby was leaning against the wall beside the door. Chrissy *wasn't* beside him. *First time tonight,* Stephanie thought.

"Got it!" she called. She held up the gray vest.

"Thanks." Bobby took it from her. "Mark and Steven took off a few minutes ago," he assured her with a grin. "They said your party was awesome." He put on his vest. "Guess it's time for me to go, too."

"Watch your step," Stephanie advised. "The porch light's burned out."

Bobby opened the door. "Walk me to the sidewalk?" he asked.

"Well—sure!" Stephanie said, surprised.

Now what's he up to? she wondered. *If he likes Chrissy, why does he want to take a walk with me?*

And a second later she thought, *I know—he's going to ask me if Chrissy likes him as much as he likes her.* She almost groaned, but managed not to.

Stephanie walked outside. Bobby didn't seem to be in a hurry. He stepped over to the left, letting the others go straight down the porch steps and onto the sidewalk. Stephanie stood beside him. The streetlights gave a little glow to the far side of the porch, but the side they were on was very dark. The night was alive with the sound of crickets.

"Uh, Steph, I really meant that I had a good time, you know," Bobby said, sounding shy. "Thanks for inviting me. I'm glad you were able to have your party, after all. Some of the kids said you weren't too sure about it earlier."

"Things . . . worked out," Stephanie said. But she was thinking frantically: *How long until D.J. gets back? Forty-five minutes? I've got to start cleaning up. I don't have time for this right now!* "I'm glad you came over."

Bobby took a deep breath. "The only thing is—well, I sort of wish I'd had some time to talk to you. That's all," he told her in a rush.

Stephanie felt a kind of electric tingle. What a sweet thing for him to say. But then she reminded herself, *Bobby likes Chrissy. He's just being polite.*

She said carefully, "I like talking to you, too."

"Thanks," Bobby said.

"Well," Stephanie replied. A few more people came out and walked away. For a few moments she and Bobby just stood there. Stephanie felt awkward. She didn't know what else to say. Maybe it would be better not to say anything at all.

"Thanks," Bobby said again. "It's fun to have a chance to hang out with someone I like and get to talk to her." He took a step toward her.

Stephanie backed away, wondering what he was doing. He took another step. He moved his face closer to hers. *Wait,* Stephanie thought. *What is he doing? Does he want to kiss me?*

"Yikes!" With his next step Bobby tripped over something. It tipped over and clattered, spilling what sounded like a hundred empty tin cans across the porch. Bobby pitched forward and landed at Stephanie's feet!

"What happened?" Stephanie asked, bending over. As she did, she bumped her head against something. "Ouch!" She felt around in the dark and grabbed hold of something made of metal. It felt like a smooth tube. It was—the handle of the lawnmower?

Bobby pushed himself up to a sitting position. "I fell over a box or something," he said. "And here's something that feels like a bowling ball!"

Stephanie took a step and nearly tripped herself. *What is all this stuff?* she wondered. *Where did it come from?*

Just then Allie opened the front door. "Steph? Where are you? Everyone's gone, and we've only got forty minutes left!"

In the light that spilled from the open door, Stephanie realized that this end of the porch was cluttered with all sorts of junk: the lawnmower, a shovel, a rake, and half a dozen boxes. The one Bobby had tripped over lay on its side. Old lighting fixtures and plumbing connections spilled out of it. And yes, right beside him was an old bowling ball!

Michelle peeked up from the corner of the porch. "Oops," she said.

Stephanie knew immediately how all that stuff had gotten there. "Michelle!" she yelled.

Chapter 11

Michelle said, "This is the last of it." She pulled an old bike frame from under the porch. Then she walked back into the storage space, where Cassie and Mandy stood, holding flashlights. Now that the storage space was empty, Michelle took a good, long look around.

She gave a sigh of disappointment. The storage space under the porch was just tall enough for her to stand up. At first, when it was crowded with all the tools and boxes, it had looked mysterious—just the place you'd want to hide a treasure.

Now Michelle realized that it was no more mysterious than the attic. Or the basement. The under-the-porch storage area was just a long, low space. The ceiling overhead was the underside of the porch. It was raw wood with a bent nail sticking through here and there. The floor was concrete.

No treasure was anywhere in sight!

Overhead the porch had creaked as lots of people walked across it. "The party must have ended," Cassie said.

"I guess so," Michelle agreed. She shook her head. "I was sure Erica's treasure was down here," she told her friends.

"Maybe she changed her mind and didn't leave it," Mandy suggested.

"Then she wouldn't have left the diary, either," Michelle pointed out. "I think—"

Crash! Something—or someone—had fallen on the porch!

"Uh-oh," Cassie said.

"I'd better check that out," Michelle said. She hurried to the door and squeezed out. She looked up onto the porch. The front door was open. In its soft glow she saw Stephanie stooping over and someone sprawled out on the porch. "Oops," she said in a small voice.

"Michelle!" Stephanie yelled.

Steph doesn't sound happy, Michelle thought. *I wonder what her problem is now? Maybe her party's turned into a disaster! Or maybe it's my bedtime!* "Uh—I'm right here," she said, as Cassie climbed out from under the porch with her flashlight.

Cassie swept the light across the porch. Cardboard boxes, gardening tools, and assorted junk were scattered everywhere. Sitting right in the middle of the mess was a tall, dark-haired guy in a gray vest.

And standing right behind him was a red-faced Stephanie. She waved her arms wildly. "What's going on?" she demanded. "What have you been up to, Michelle? Where did all this—this *stuff* come from?"

Michelle blinked. "Well, it started out under the porch," she explained. "Cassie and Mandy and I had to drag it out. We just moved it up onto the porch so it would be safe—"

"Safe!" Stephanie exclaimed, squinting in

the flashlight's glare. "It's right at the edge of the porch! And the light's burned out! Didn't you know that someone could fall and get hurt?"

"I'm not hurt," the guy said mildly. "Really, I'm okay."

"I didn't think about that," Michelle confessed in a small voice.

"Why?" Stephanie wailed. "Why are you doing all this?"

Michelle wondered how Stephanie could keep forgetting important things like her treasure hunt. Then she realized, *Maybe Steph's upset because her party got out of hand. That could explain a lot.*

It would be best to explain everything calmly and slowly, Michelle decided. "We had to move this stuff out so we could look for Erica's treasure," she reminded her sister. "See, we searched everywhere else where there's no window. That was the clue, remember? Well, we went through every closet and the attic and the basement. So this is about the last place left that doesn't have a window of light. So it almost *had* to be under the—"

Michelle stopped talking when she saw that Stephanie wasn't paying attention. She had stooped over and was helping the boy get to his feet. "Look what you did to Bobby," she scolded. "He might have broken his neck."

"No, I'm cool," Bobby returned. He kicked his foot to untangle a coil of copper pipe from his right ankle. It fell off and rolled a little way, then rattled down the stairs like a rolling penny. "No bones broken. Really, it's no big deal."

Stephanie started throwing things back into the box with clangs and bangs and clatters. "I'm sorry, Bobby," she said. Michelle thought her sister was about to burst into tears. "This night has turned into a total mess."

"Uh, Steph," Darcy asked from the doorway. She held up the receiver of the cordless phone. "Can you take a phone call?"

Stephanie raised her arms and let them drop to her sides. "Sure. Why not?" Michelle bit her lip. It sounded as if Steph had just given up. It was as if she were saying, "The worst has already happened. What next?"

Darcy handed Stephanie the phone.

113

Maybe this treasure hunt wasn't such a hot idea, Michelle thought. *I didn't mean for anyone to fall. And I forgot the porch light isn't working. But I just know Erica meant for someone like me to find her treasure. If I can just get Stephanie to see things my way—*

Stephanie was talking into the receiver. "Hello. Oh . . . sure, fine!" Her voice was high and fast. She sounded almost as if she had been running. "Really, just fine. Okay. Okay. That's . . . that's cool. Right. See you."

She sank down on the edge of the porch. "I was wrong before. *Now* this night is a total mess. That was D.J. Her seminar's over, and after she stops at the store, she'll be right home. She'll be here in half an hour!"

"That's perfect," Michelle said, trying to cheer up Steph. "She can help us put all this stuff back. I mean, there's a lot to do and just you and me—"

Stephanie gave her a wild-eyed look. "Omigosh!" She jumped to her feet. "Half an hour. We've got to get things back to normal before D.J. shows up. Bobby, um, it's been really nice. See you on Monday."

"Wait," Bobby said. "I'll help."

"Help?" Stephanie repeated. "That's what I need. Help!" She tossed the phone back to Darcy and added, "Darcy, get Allie on the double. We've got to clean this place up. Let's get started." She dashed back into the house.

"Hi," Bobby said, waving at Michelle.

"Hi," Michelle replied. "Uh, that's my sister. She gets a little excited sometimes."

"Tell me about it," Bobby agreed. "Okay, what do we have to do?"

"I guess we've got to get this stuff back under the porch," Michelle said.

Bobby picked up the box Stephanie had repacked. "Okay. Let's get started." He came rattling down the steps with the box as Michelle, Mandy, and Cassie collected gardening tools.

With Bobby's help, it took only about five minutes to move the stuff back under the porch. The hard part was wrestling the lawnmower down, but Bobby did that for them.

He's really nice, Michelle thought, as Bobby wheeled the lawnmower through the doorway under the porch. *I don't see why Steph couldn't like someone like him.*

They shoved a few more things in, and then Michelle looked everything over in the glow of a flashlight. *It isn't all in the same place as before*, she realized, *but maybe no one will notice. It was kind of cluttered, anyway. And at least we got everything out of sight.*

Then Mandy nudged Michelle. "Hey, Michelle? I was just wondering. Do you think Stephanie's going to mind the mess we made in the bedrooms?"

"*All* the bedrooms?" Cassie put in helpfully.

"And the living room?" Mandy added. "And . . . sort of everywhere? We tossed a lot of stuff around."

Cassie went on, "And we didn't put anything back. Is that going to get Stephanie in trouble?"

The question hit Michelle hard. *They're right*, she thought. *D.J. sort of left Steph in charge. I'm going to get in trouble, but so is Steph! She didn't take care of the house very well.*

"We'll have to help," Michelle decided. "Come on, guys." She looked up at Bobby hopefully. "You wouldn't want to . . . help a little more, would you?"

"No problem," Bobby said. "Tell you what. I'll go ask Stephanie what I need to do."

Michelle and her friends hurried inside. First they went down to the basement apartment. "This won't be too hard," Michelle said, lugging an armload of Joey's clothes to the closet. "They weren't neat to begin with!" She started to hang up trousers and shirts. Joey didn't seem to keep them in any particular order.

"It's your dad's closet I'm worried about," Cassie said. She tossed Joey's shoes back into the closet.

Mandy hung up sports jackets and ties. After a couple of minutes, the place didn't look *too* bad. "What's next?" Mandy asked Michelle.

"The storage area under the stairs," Michelle ordered. "Hurry!"

They ran back upstairs. Bobby was running the vacuum cleaner in the living room. Michelle grinned. It was really nice of him to pitch in. She and Cassie and Mandy got to work, too. They stuffed a ventriloquist doll, clown trousers, and lots of other stuff under the stairs. "That doesn't go!" Michelle yelped when she saw Cassie about to toss a cushion in. "That belongs on the sofa. Did we pick up everything?"

Mandy turned around. She was wearing a pair of glasses that had a fake nose, moustache, and eyebrows glued to it. "Looks like it."

"Put those in, too." Michelle tried not to giggle. "We don't have time to play. We've got to get upstairs!"

"We never finished searching for Erica's treasure," Mandy complained as she threw the glasses into the storage space and shut the sticky door.

"We didn't even find a trapdoor or secret panel," Cassie agreed.

Stephanie rushed into the living room. She was carrying a tall stack of CDs. She ran past Bobby, stopped, and turned. Her mouth was open. "Bobby, you don't have to do that," she said.

Bobby switched off the vacuum. "It's no trouble. I can stay for half an hour longer," he offered. "I don't mind. It won't make me *that* late getting home. Just tell me what we need."

"We need a plan of action," Stephanie shot back. She paused a moment, the stack of CDs in her hands wobbling. To Michelle it looked as if her sister were thinking as fast as the wheels in her head could spin.

Allie and Darcy were also in the living room, working hard. Darcy was carrying a bulging garbage bag. Allie was scooping soda cans into the recycling bin.

Finally Stephanie said, "We've got twenty minutes. Maybe a little more, because D.J.'s going to the store. Okay, Darce, you put the CDs back into the rack. Allie, you make sure everything on this floor is back in place. Bobby, could you dump the garbage and put the recycling bin on the curb, then come with me to the kitchen? That's where the biggest mess is. I'll start loading the dishwasher. Michelle, Cassie, Mandy, clean up every mess you made!"

"We're working on it," Michelle told her. "We just finished this, and now we're going up to our room."

"Great," Stephanie said. "No, wait. Leave our room and the attic until tomorrow. Nobody will notice them! Start on D.J.'s room, then go to Dad's. Move, move, move!"

"We're on it," Bobby said. "What else do we need to do?"

Michelle knew. "We need to find a miracle!"

STEPHANIE

Chapter
12

That's the last dish," Bobby told Stephanie, as he handed her a dirty plate.

Stephanie quickly rinsed the plate in the sink. Then she found a slot for it in the dishwasher. It was a tight fit. Even with all the plastic cups and plates, the kids at the party had used almost every dish in the house. At least nothing had been broken.

Stephanie shut the dishwasher door and switched the machine on. "Thanks," she said, leaning back against the counter and brushing her hair back from her face.

Bobby grabbed a sponge and cleaned up

the spilled soda on the stove and floor. "Yup," he said, "you can definitely tell when Arnett and Pascoe have been to a party."

Stephanie couldn't help smiling. "Bobby, you've helped enough. I'll get the rest. You need to go home now."

"You sure?" Bobby asked. "Your friends are pretty fast at cleanup detail, but there's a lot to do. I'll stay a little longer if you need me."

Stephanie smiled and shook her head. "We'll manage. I think the six of us can get a handle on things."

"Well," Bobby said. "If you're sure."

He's been great, Stephanie thought. *Lots of guys would have just sailed out the door. But Bobby stayed and pitched right in to help!*

"Hey, it was really nice of you to help Michelle and her friends put that stuff back under the porch," she told him. "And vacuuming the living room improved things a lot. And thanks for helping me with this disaster area."

Bobby grinned. Stephanie swept her gaze around the kitchen. Now that the floor was swept, the counters cleared, and the dishes cleaned up, it didn't look bad. And most of the party food was gone. The kids had eaten all the chips, crackers, dip, cheese, and nuts. They had gone through almost all the sodas.

The only real survivor of the party was a little more than a foot of the gigantic hero sandwich. It stuck out of its long cellophane wrapper, looking lonely.

The sandwich, Stephanie thought. *The second D.J. sees it, she'll start to ask questions.*

Stephanie pointed to the hero. "Maybe there *is* something you could do. Want to eat that?"

Smiling, Bobby shook his head. "I think I already ate three feet of it at the party," he told her. "Hey, you've still got some stuff to do. I don't want to be in the way. I guess I'll go now if you've got everything under control."

"I've got *nothing* under control," Stephanie admitted. "But if I keep going, we might get past D.J. Hey, Bobby?"

Bobby looked at her expectantly. His expression was a little shy. "Yeah?"

Stephanie felt herself blushing with embarrassment. "Well, I was just going to say that, even with the problems, I'm glad we got to spend a little time together. Even if it was kitchen patrol."

"That's the whole reason I came here," Bobby admitted, breaking into a grin. "To hang with you, I mean. I've wanted to do that since our first day in biology class!"

Stephanie couldn't believe her ears. "I figured you were here tonight to talk to Chrissy," she admitted.

Bobby's face turned red. "I guess I did talk to Chrissy a lot. But that was because I was kind of pressing her for information."

Stephanie raised her eyebrows at him. "Information?" she echoed. "About what?"

"About you!" Bobby told her. In a rushed voice he went on, "I think you're, you know, pretty cool. I've noticed you a lot in bio, but we couldn't talk in class, and when class ended, you always had to run. Anyway, I was talking to Chrissy because—"

He broke off and took a deep breath. "I sort of wanted to know if you had a boyfriend or if maybe you and I could go out sometime, you know?"

Stephanie's heart pounded. So that was why Bobby and Chrissy had had their heads together all night! She laughed in relief. "Well, I don't have a boyfriend," she said. Her stomach fluttered with butterflies. "And I would like to hang out with you. Anytime."

"Great," Bobby replied. He looked away and in a soft voice he murmured, "That's totally cool."

"Anytime," Stephanie repeated. "Only, right now I'm running *out* of time!"

A frazzled-looking Darcy poked her head in the doorway. "Sixteen minutes!" She popped back out again, like a cuckoo disappearing into its clock.

"Oh, right, you're busy. I'd better go," Bobby told Stephanie. "But it *is* okay if I call you, right?"

"Sure," Stephanie said, smiling. "It's *extremely* okay."

She walked him to the front porch.

Bobby turned under the streetlight and waved. He had a big grin on his face. Stephanie waved back.

Then she turned and flew back into the

house. Bobby wanted to hang out with her! She sighed happily.

How cool is that? she asked herself.

But she didn't stop to think about it for very long. She didn't have time for that. Darcy's warning echoed in her mind. Sixteen minutes until D.J. came home. And there was still serious cleaning to do!

Stephanie saw Darcy run up the stairs with an armload of CDs. Allie came the other way, running down the steps with an armload of CDs. They passed each other, stopped, turned, and did a double take. "I've been hauling these up to Steph's room!" Darcy yelped.

"No wonder I couldn't finish bringing them down!" Allie said. She turned to Stephanie. "Steph, up or down?"

"You go upstairs and put yours in my room. Darcy, put yours in the living room. I'll sort them out tomorrow. Right now, the living room rack just has to look full when D.J. gets home. Go, go, go!"

Stephanie hurried upstairs. Everything

looked okay on the landing. She peeked into D.J.'s room. Good news there, she saw. The girls had already replaced her clothes in the closet—*I hope it's halfway neat!* Stephanie thought. *I'd better check, just to be safe.*

A quick glance into D.J.'s closet showed Stephanie that it was at least roughly in order. D.J. kept all her casual clothes on the left and the dressy ones on the right. Right next to the ventriloquist's dummy.

Ventriloquist's dummy? That's not D.J.'s, it's Joey's! Stephanie grabbed the floppy doll. She darted onto the landing and almost ran into Michelle's friend Cassie.

"There's Joey's dummy. We've been looking all over for it," Cassie said.

"I found it in D.J.'s closet," Stephanie told her. "Right beside her favorite dress. How'd it get there?"

Cassie took the dummy and scratched her head. "Well, we tossed it out of Joey's storage space under the stairs. I guess somebody at the party must have brought it upstairs. Then I must have picked it up and when we were putting D.J.'s stuff back in her closet, I must have hung it up by mistake! I'll stuff it back under the stairs!"

"Where's Michelle?" Stephanie called as Cassie hurried down to the living room.

"She and Mandy are going to be in your dad's room in a minute!" Cassie yelled back. "We've still got all of his stuff to put away."

Danny's room! Stephanie rushed there. She groaned as soon as she opened the door. Danny was truly a neat freak. With just one glance, he would be able to tell that someone had disturbed his closet.

Well, it couldn't be helped. *We didn't break anything,* Stephanie told herself. *It's not like anything is ruined. But he's going to ask some serious questions!*

Maybe she and Michelle could tell him they were looking for stuff for a craft project. Or they could say they messed up his closet while looking for old shirts to wear while painting. She could figure out what they actually painted later. Maybe they could even think of something they *could* paint, so it wouldn't be a fib!

As Stephanie started to hang up Danny's

shirts, Michelle and Mandy came in. "Hey, thanks, Steph," Michelle said. "You're doing a great job!"

"Come and help," Stephanie told her. She looked at the cluttered floor and shook her head. "Do you remember how the shoes were arranged?"

To Stephanie's surprise Michelle whipped out a piece of paper. She unfolded it and began to read aloud: "Okay, this goes from left to right. Black wingtips, black loafers, black tassel loafers—"

"You made a *chart*?" Stephanie asked, amazed.

Michelle gave her a look. "This is Dad we're talking about. I *had* to make a chart!"

Soon Cassie came back and pitched in. The four of them worked hard, and in less than five minutes, Danny's closet looked perfect. *Well*, Stephanie thought, *maybe not perfect, but at least in reasonably good shape.* If they were very lucky, there was a chance their dad wouldn't notice the changes.

Stephanie, Michelle, Cassie, and Mandy took one more sweep through the bedrooms, then decided they had time to do the attic apartment. Luckily, Uncle Jesse and Aunt Becky were much more easygoing about order and tidiness than Danny. With the twins around they *had* to be. Filling up their closets was easy for the girls. They simply used the grab and stuff method!

They came clattering down the stairs to find Darcy putting away a broom and Allie lugging the last garbage bag out of the living room. "Think this will do?" Allie asked from the doorway.

Stephanie took a quick look around. "Maybe." *It doesn't look too bad,* she thought. *The sofa cushions aren't quite right, and the CD rack doesn't have the right CDs in it. But it's just sort of jumbled, not dirty. Maybe like the six of us were snacking and lounging around, watching TV—*

"Michelle!" she yelled. "Quick, turn on the TV!"

Michelle grabbed the remote from the sofa. She found a music channel. A rock video blared out of the TV. It was one of the weird ones, with everything from ballerinas bowling to tropical fish swimming in midair.

Stephanie looked at her watch. "A minute to spare. We're home free!"

"Hey, guys!" Allie yelled from the kitchen. "What about this?"

They all dashed inside. "What?" Stephanie demanded. "What is it?"

"It's the sandwich!" Allie said. She took the last foot of bulging hero sandwich from its long wrapper. "Should we toss it?"

Michelle looked at Stephanie. "Dad hates it if we waste good food," she reminded her sister.

"Put it in the fridge?" Darcy suggested.

Allie shook her head. "No way. D.J. would be sure to see it there."

"That leaves us just one option," Stephanie said. "Eat it. Who's hungry?"

Michelle wrinkled her nose. "I don't *like* those things. But I guess I could eat a little."

Allie held the hero up. "This is still a *big* sandwich. It's not only long, it's thick. It's crammed with cold cuts and cheese and—"

"Don't do a commercial. Just chow down. Everybody!" Stephanie commanded. She retrieved a bread knife and sliced off six

131

pieces of sandwich. When she finished, there was still a thick piece left.

"Good sandwich," Mandy mumbled as she munched. "Lots of veggies."

"Mmm," agreed Cassie.

"Should I *chew*?" Darcy asked, holding up her slice of sandwich. "Or just try to *inhale* it, like the boys do?"

Stephanie swallowed. She wasn't the least bit hungry. The bite seemed to take forever going down. With a gasp, she said, "We can't possibly eat it all. We can't finish it in one minute. We need another miracle!"

"I think we're out of miracles," Darcy said. "And your sister's due home right this second!"

"Maybe we need something *besides* a miracle!" Michelle said. "I think I know just what we need!" And then she yelled, "Comet, here, boy! Hey, Comet!"

A few minutes later the girls were back in the living room. Stephanie felt exhausted. The others looked just about as tired as she felt.

"D.J.'s late," Michelle observed.

"Thank goodness," Stephanie told her. "At least we've had time to catch our breath."

Allie, Darcy, and Stephanie had flopped onto the sofa. Mandy, Cassie, and Michelle were sitting on the floor in front of the TV. From the kitchen the happy sound of Comet gobbling the rest of the sandwich had finally stopped.

Then Stephanie sat up straight. She heard a car engine outside. D.J.!

And Stephanie had just noticed a pair of big floppy red clown shoes perched on top of a bookcase. She leaped up, grabbed them, and spun around as the car stopped outside. Darcy understood what was happening. She jumped off the couch and tugged at the door to the storage space under the stairs. "It's stuck again!" she yelled.

Stephanie looked around wildly. She heard the car door slam outside. Quickly she shoved the shoes under the sofa and collapsed in her corner again as Darcy jumped over the couch and sat down on the cushion next to her.

The doorknob rattled and D.J. walked in. She was carrying a big brown grocery bag. "Hi, guys," she said. "Sorry I'm a little late!"

"Oh, that's okay," Stephanie said. *Whew!* she thought. *That was* close. Her eyes darted around the living room. *Hope we didn't overlook anything else.*

D.J. held up the bag she was carrying. "Maybe this will make up for it. I bought lots of goodies at the store. Popcorn and cookies and other munchies. You're probably all starving, so dig right in."

Stephanie's stomach lurched. "Umm . . . thanks. Maybe later. We've been sort of snacking already, so . . . uhh . . ." She knew she had to change the subject fast. "So, how was your seminar?"

D.J. shrugged. "Could've been dull, but Dr. Overberg has a good sense of humor. He kept things rolling along. There were lots of questions at the end. That's one thing that made me late." She sat in an armchair. "Man, am I glad to be home. How were things here tonight?"

"Fine," Stephanie chirped. She realized right away that her eyes were a little too wide and her voice sounded a little too high. She swallowed hard. Her sister was sure to notice that something was up.

D.J. gave her a suspicious look. "Steph? You sound pretty cheerful, considering. I mean, I *did* spoil your party plans, so what—"

"But we had a good time all by ourselves," Michelle put in helpfully. "The six of us. Just sort of, you know, uh, hanging out and stuff."

"Yeah, it was pretty . . . uneventful," Darcy said.

"Dull," Cassie added. "But *fun* dull."

D.J. tilted her head. "Fun dull? What are you all talking about? What did you six do this evening?"

Stephanie was thinking furiously. *What can I tell her, without telling a lie?* She waved her hands. "We listened to music."

Michelle nodded. "We, uh, snacked. And we rearranged our closets."

Mandy started to laugh. Stephanie shot her a warning look. Mandy turned it into a cough.

"We watched TV," Cassie offered. "Uh, maybe we had it turned up kind of loud earlier. So if any of your neighbors heard music, it might have been the TV."

D.J. stood up. "Steph," she said in a serious voice, "is there something that you need to tell me about? Something that went on here tonight?"

Oh, no! Stephanie thought. *What can I say?* She tried to look innocent. "Umm . . . no, I don't think so," she said carefully.

D.J. still didn't look satisfied. For a moment she just stared at Stephanie. "You'd tell me if anything really bad had happened, right?" she asked.

Stephanie nodded firmly. "You know I would."

"Okay, then," D.J. decided. "I know I can trust you. So we can just leave it at—" She broke off, staring toward the kitchen.

Stephanie turned.

Comet was prancing into the living room.

He was dragging something. It was a five-foot-long strip of colored cellophane. In big blue letters the cellophane read, "Hoagie S. Grinder's Super Sub Special."

Stephanie groaned. *Just when I thought it was over*, she told herself. *We're busted!*

Chapter
13

Oh, no! Michelle thought. Comet trotted across the living room, dragging the five-foot-long sandwich wrapper behind him. He took the wrapper straight to D.J.

"And what is this?" D.J. asked, taking the cellophane from the dog. She held it up and looked at the label. "A Hoagie S. Grinder's Super Sub Special? All right, Stephanie, where did *this* come from?"

For a moment no one spoke. Allie and Darcy sighed. Mandy and Cassie looked at Michelle.

Michelle looked at Stephanie. She realized

137

that her sister had no good answer. Thinking very fast, Michelle said, "Uh, D.J., the sandwich was kinda my fault. We were looking for the hidden surprise—"

Stephanie gave her a thankful glance, but D.J. frowned. "A surprise hidden in a sandwich?" she demanded.

Michelle shook her head. "No, no. Remember Erica?"

D.J.'s puzzled frown deepened. "Who's Erica?"

"Erica!" Michelle repeated. "The little girl who used to live in our house ages ago? The one whose diary I found upstairs in the attic? She wrote a poem about a surprise that she hid for someone to find."

D.J. nodded. "Oh, right. What about her?"

"Well, I kind of invited, uh, everyone to join in the treasure hunt," Michelle explained. "We had to look all over the house for Erica's surprise. We knew we'd get hungry, so we talked Steph into ordering a sandwich."

"You have to have lots of energy for a treasure hunt," Mandy added.

"Right," Michelle said quickly. "And a

sandwich like that gives you all the energy you need!"

D.J. looked totally amazed. She held up the wrapper and let it dangle. It was almost as tall as she was! Comet sniffed the open end of the wrapper as if he suspected more sandwich was lurking there. But D.J. just shook her head. "A five-foot-long Super Sub hero sandwich?" she asked. "You ordered it for just the six of you?"

"Mmm!" Darcy said. "It was *sooooo* good!"

Cassie smacked her lips. "You know how it is with great food. We just couldn't stop eating!"

"In fact, I think maybe we ate a little *too* much," Mandy put in.

Michelle stared at D.J. Was she going to buy the story? She didn't look fully convinced, but at last she smiled. "Okay, okay," she said. She crumpled up the wrapper into a ball. "I think I know the *real* reason you guys had a sub sandwich here!"

Stephanie's head dropped. She looked so sad that Michelle thought she was going to cry. In a small voice Stephanie asked, "You do?"

D.J. laughed. "Sure," she said, and to

Michelle she didn't sound upset at all. "Steph, you ordered it for the party, didn't you? I'll bet you forgot to cancel the order. Right?"

Michelle jumped up. "Yes! That's it! Steph *did* order it for the party, but since there wasn't going to *be* a party, we ate it ourselves."

D.J. shook her head. "And you thought you had to eat it so I wouldn't be upset? Steph, you paid for it with your own money! I wouldn't have given you a hard time about something like that."

"Thanks," Stephanie said. She seemed to be talking to D.J., but Michelle thought the message was really for her.

D.J. tossed the balled-up wrapper from hand to hand. "These sandwiches are *enormous*. I don't know why you're not all sick! But I guess there's no harm done. No wonder you don't want snacks!"

"Not for a long time," Allie moaned.

D.J. turned to Michelle. "Tell me, how did your treasure hunt turn out? Did you find Erica's surprise?"

Michelle's mood sank a little. She shook her

head glumly. "We never did. And we looked *everywhere*."

Stephanie's face showed her relief at getting off the hook with D.J. "Tell us the clue again, Michelle," she said. "I'm not sure I remember it all."

Sighing, Michelle ran to their room and brought the red diary back down. "Here it is," she told everyone, and she read the poem out loud:

There's something in storage,
Locked up tight,
In the place without a window of light.
If you can find it,
Then you will see,
A present there to you from me.

She finished and glanced around. Nobody looked inspired.

"We know it isn't in a closet, or the attic or basement. Or under the stairs or the place under the porch," Michelle told D.J. "We searched all those places. I don't know where else to look."

"Hmmm. I wonder why she even mentioned a window," D.J. said softly.

Maybe D.J. has a point, Michelle thought. *Maybe Erica meant that a window was close to the place.* But she couldn't figure out what that place might be.

"Well," D.J. said, "our history lecturer told us most problems can be solved if you think about them logically. Erica was about Michelle's age when she hid her surprise, right?"

"She was eleven years old," Michelle said. "Just a little older than I am."

D.J. nodded. "Then, Michelle, if *you* wanted to hide something in this house, where would you put it?"

Michelle shrugged. "I dunno. Steph?"

Everyone looked at Stephanie. "If it was me," she started slowly, "I'd definitely hide it in my room. Think about it. Of all the rooms in the house, that's the one I know best."

"Which room did Erica sleep in?" D.J. wondered.

Michelle flipped through the diary. "I think it was *our* room." She found the page she was looking for. "Right here she talks about how the sun shines in her window. That's just the way it comes in through our bedroom window."

"A window of light!" Allie exclaimed.

"The window!" Stephanie and Michelle shouted at the same moment. They gave each other an excited look.

Could it be? Michelle wondered.

"Michelle, there *is* another storage space in our room besides the closet!" Stephanie insisted.

"One close to a window, too!" D.J. put in.

"You're right!" Michelle squealed. "Come on, everyone!" She sped toward the stairs, her pulse pounding. This time she was sure she knew where the secret treasure was hidden!

Michelle dashed upstairs to her room, with the others following close behind. She ran straight to the window with its cozy window seat underneath. "This is it!" she cried. "Here's the window of light! And under it is the window seat!"

"I don't get it," Cassie protested.

"It's not *just* a place to sit," Michelle told

her. "Look!" She tossed the cushions aside and tugged. The seat flipped up on hidden hinges. It revealed a little opening, almost like a small trunk. "This is a storage space! I'll bet Erica used to put her toys and stuff in here!"

"*We* used to put our toys in there," Stephanie agreed. "Check it out, Michelle!"

Michelle took out a couple of old teddy bears and some doll clothes. But the compartment under the seat was pretty small—and now it was empty.

"Nothing," Michelle reported, feeling her spirits dip again. "And this time I was so sure."

Stephanie frowned. "I may be wrong. It's been a long time since I kept stuff in there. But I seem to remember one of the boards on the bottom always felt a little loose. Push on them and see if one wobbles!"

Michelle bent over and shoved. The bottom of the compartment was made of three boards. And when she pushed the board in the center, she felt the wood give! "Yes!" she yelled. "The middle board wiggles! How do we get it out?"

Stephanie dropped to her knees beside Michelle. "Push on one end. If you can make the other end come up a little, I'll try to snag it!"

Michelle rocked and shoved. The board wiggled and wobbled. Finally a corner of it came up, just an inch or two. Steph caught it with her fingernails. "See if you can get the edge!" she told Michelle.

Michelle's smaller fingers could just grip the board. She tugged and felt it swing up a little more. It was a tight fit, and the board was really jammed in, but at last it came free with a squeak.

"There's something under it!" Michelle announced, seeing the gleam of metal.

"Dig it out!" Stephanie encouraged her.

Michelle reached into the smaller opening. She could feel something round. The top seemed to be flat. She worked it out and saw that she was holding a round gold-colored cookie tin. On its lid was a faded label made from a three-by-five note card held to the tin by yellowed tape. In faint purple letters the label read, TIME CAPSULE.

"Cool!" Mandy exclaimed, as Michelle lowered her prize to the floor.

Cassie was excited, too. "That could be Erica's treasure chest," she said. "Let's see what's inside!"

Michelle's heart pounded with excitement. She worked at the lid. It had rusted a little and was hard to remove. Finally, though, it popped off and clattered to the floor.

All seven girls bent over the open treasure tin. Michelle scooped out a handful of black-and-white photos. Each one had writing on the back.

"This is why the photo album we found in the attic was empty," Michelle said softly. "All the photographs are here."

She began to look through them. DAD AND MOM showed a young, smiling couple standing in front of an old-fashioned car. ME was a photo of a cheerful-looking blond-haired girl about six years old. She was missing two front teeth, and she wore her long hair in two pigtails. Another photo was ME AND JESSICA. It showed the same blond girl, but a few years older—maybe eight, Michelle thought. She was holding the hand of an older girl, who looked to be about twelve.

"She said she had an older sister named Jessica," Michelle observed. "And Jessica looks about four years older than Erica, just like you're four years older than I am, Steph."

"Neat," Stephanie said. She picked up another photo. "Oh, look—here's our room!"

Michelle grinned. It was strange, seeing her room the way it looked all those years ago. The walls were painted with what looked like puffy clouds. A circus poster hung on the wall where Steph's bed now was. And on the window seat sat a huge stuffed teddy bear, its button eyes gleaming.

Other photos showed the neighborhood. The trees were all smaller, and the cars were old-fashioned. There were even five shots of Erica's family trip to New York, with funny roundish-looking taxicabs in the background. The women wore long dresses and tiny little hats.

I almost got it right when I made my drawing, Michelle thought proudly. *My taxi looks just like the ones in the picture!*

"There's one thing left in the cookie tin," Stephanie pointed out. "Michelle, see what it is."

Michelle took out a folded piece of paper. It had something flat and hard inside. She tried to unfold it and discovered it was an envelope. It had been sealed and then folded again and again. Michelle tore it open. A gleaming gold chain fell into her hand. From it a heart dangled—a heart with a zigzag break down the middle. "What's this?" she asked.

D.J. took it and smiled. "I know what this is. It's a friendship necklace. You take one half of the heart and give the other half to your best friend. As long as you wear your half and she wears hers, you're always connected."

Michelle saw a second gold chain in the envelope. She took it out. "Maybe you and Steph should have the pieces of the heart," she said, offering the chain to D.J.

D.J. shook her head. "Thanks, Michelle, but you found it. I think you and Steph should share it."

"Okay, Steph?" Michelle asked.

"You know it is," Stephanie replied with a smile.

Michelle took half the heart off the first necklace and put it on the second one. "This is so cool, and it gives me a great idea. D.J., can we make a time capsule for the next family that lives in this house?"

D.J. laughed. "I think that would be a totally cool thing to do. As long as you don't stuff a giant submarine sandwich in there."

"We'll make it together," Stephanie offered. "All of us. You, me, D.J., and our friends."

"Great idea," Michelle told her. She held out a necklace with half the heart on it. "And this is for you, Steph. For being such a great sister."

"Thanks," Stephanie said with a wink, as she put the necklace on. "You know something? When we work together, we *always* do a good job!"

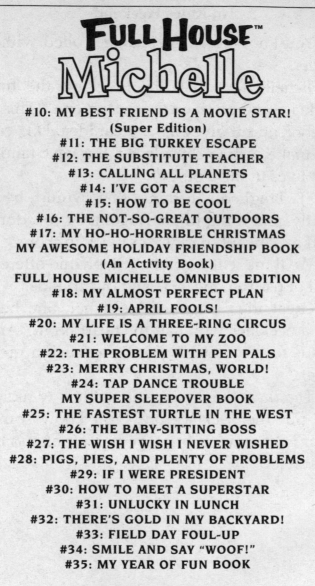

FULL HOUSE™
Michelle

#10: MY BEST FRIEND IS A MOVIE STAR!
(Super Edition)
#11: THE BIG TURKEY ESCAPE
#12: THE SUBSTITUTE TEACHER
#13: CALLING ALL PLANETS
#14: I'VE GOT A SECRET
#15: HOW TO BE COOL
#16: THE NOT-SO-GREAT OUTDOORS
#17: MY HO-HO-HORRIBLE CHRISTMAS
MY AWESOME HOLIDAY FRIENDSHIP BOOK
(An Activity Book)
FULL HOUSE MICHELLE OMNIBUS EDITION
#18: MY ALMOST PERFECT PLAN
#19: APRIL FOOLS!
#20: MY LIFE IS A THREE-RING CIRCUS
#21: WELCOME TO MY ZOO
#22: THE PROBLEM WITH PEN PALS
#23: MERRY CHRISTMAS, WORLD!
#24: TAP DANCE TROUBLE
MY SUPER SLEEPOVER BOOK
#25: THE FASTEST TURTLE IN THE WEST
#26: THE BABY-SITTING BOSS
#27: THE WISH I WISH I NEVER WISHED
#28: PIGS, PIES, AND PLENTY OF PROBLEMS
#29: IF I WERE PRESIDENT
#30: HOW TO MEET A SUPERSTAR
#31: UNLUCKY IN LUNCH
#32: THERE'S GOLD IN MY BACKYARD!
#33: FIELD DAY FOUL-UP
#34: SMILE AND SAY "WOOF!"
#35: MY YEAR OF FUN BOOK

A MINSTREL® BOOK
Published by Pocket Books
™ & © 2000 Warner Bros. All Rights Reserved.

1033-34

*Don't miss out on any of
Stephanie and Michelle's
exciting adventures!*

FULL HOUSE™
Sisters

*When sisters get together...
expect the unexpected!*

A MINSTREL® BOOK
Published by Pocket Books

2012-05